THE HEALER

PRAKRITI KANDEL

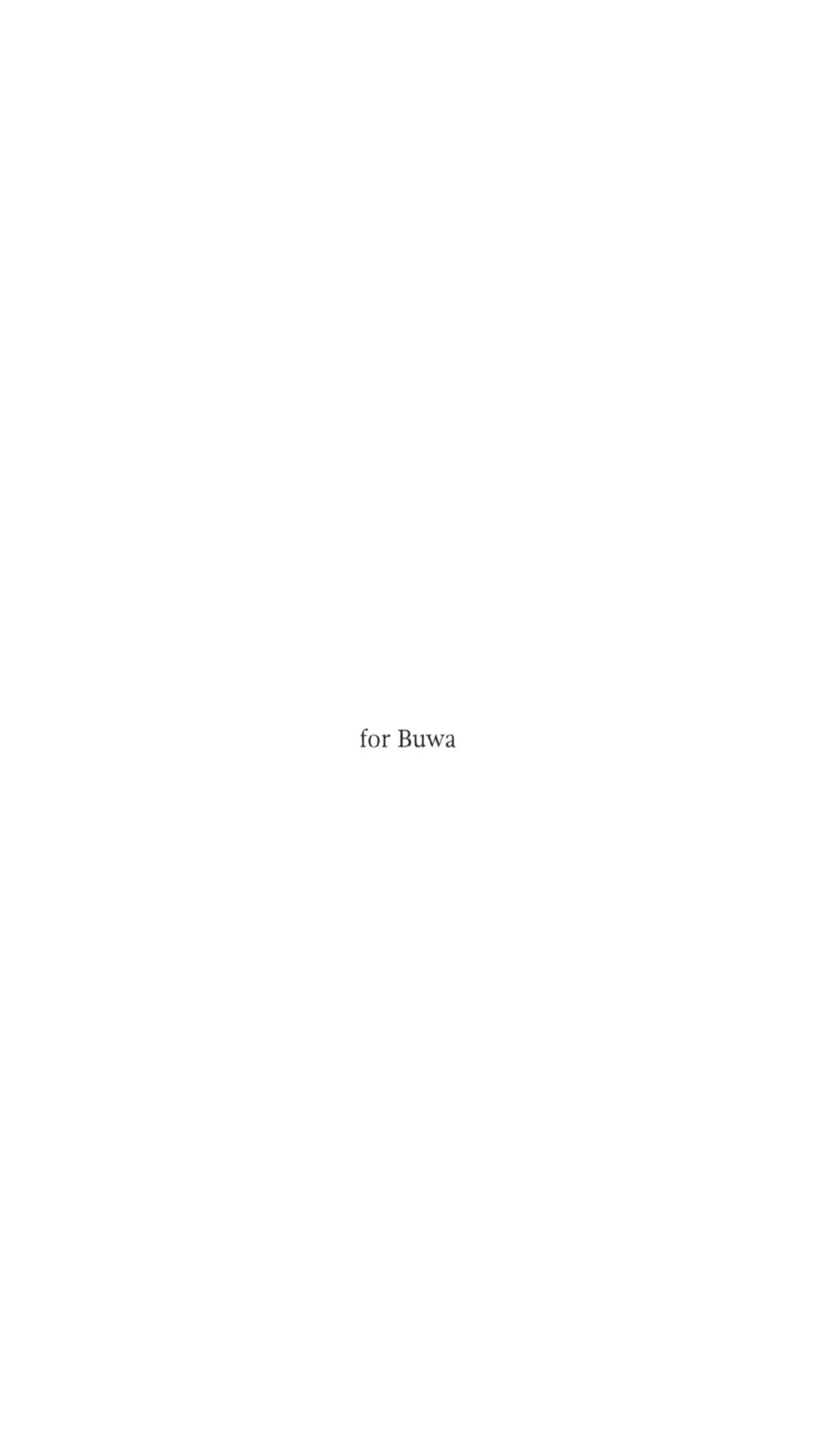

for Buwa

Contents

CHAPTER ONE

RIVER

Inside her study room, Amrita plucked up the thick roll of paper she had received yesterday from where she had placed it on the bookshelf. She walked to the couch by the window and sank in it, placing the paper on the low square table in front. Outside, it was a winter morning, but the sun had imprinted its warm presence onto the sky. Sunlight filtered in through the window's metal frame and colliding against the furniture, fell on the wooden floor. Back at the table, Amrita's roll of paper lay partly in sunlight and partly in shadows. Briskly switching out of her relaxed posture, Amrita leaned over the table and rolled the paper open— slowly— like a delicate, precious parchment. Inside, there was a letter first, which she had read yesterday. She put the letter aside, and focused on the paper below. It was a map.

Amrita studied the map's encircled part. It was a forest north-east, perhaps a hundred kilometers above A name was printed in tiny letters— Shankhachowki. Prominent flowing lines beside the forest showed a river. *So it was a riverbank where Kalpana wanted to meet.* Amrita traced her finger from the encircled riverbank to her current location. Retrieving a ruler from her study table, she measured the distance, and with help from the scale at the bottom, she calculated exactly how far this place was. Then, she closed her eyes and focused on the riverside in Shankhachowki and on Kalpana. A vision of Kalpana bending to touch the water flashed in her mind. "So she's there." Amrita whispered to herself.

Carrying the map and the letter inside her coat's pocket, Amrita walked out of the room. She was already dressed so she went down the stairs, and out the front door. Despite the sun's early effort, it had not succeeded in separating the air's attachment with the cold. Amrita pulled her coat tighter around her body. In the garden, the flowers had diminished in the winter– there were spots of marigold left over from the autumn and stems of poinsettia rose to the sky and added some vibrance with their bright red and green leaves. The more delicate flowers had withered by now, and the grass was much more arid compared to the monsoon when it would be perennially moist with the rainwater it absorbed. Opening her front gate, Amrita stepped into the forest. Apart from occasional voices of birds in the distance, a serene silence rang through the trees, whose leaves flurried slightly in the cold air. These majestic trees were her most rooted friends and neighbors. Apart from Amrita's two-story cottage, there was no other house in sight. Amrita walked for fifteen minutes through the forest and stopped, surrounded by trees in all directions.

She took a deep breath in. Raising her hands, she cast a protective spell around her. It was a transparent barrier, but no one could see her now. When traveling, she preferred to be amidst trees— their tall, tranquil trunks imbued her with a deeper sense of calm than being at home— even though her cottage was invisible to others.

She closed her eyes and thought about the location she had seen in her vision minutes ago, where Kalpana had been. Her mind was immediately transported to the forest by the riverbank. She focused until she felt all her energy exist in that place. Waving her hand, she said, "*Yatrayam.*"

The next minute, when Amrita opened her eyes, she was there by the riverbank— the sound of the river's powerful flowing motion filled the air. Kalpana, who had been bending over the river, turned behind, squinting her bright, deep-brown eyes as the morning light fell on her face. Kalpana was dressed in a long, woolen kurtha threaded with golden patterns and had a coat flung over her shoulders. Her black hair, which fell to her shoulders, was meticulously plaited behind. Every time Amrita saw Kalpana, from that first moment six years ago, she felt a warm glow inside her— like everything would be fine. Amrita walked towards her.

"How are you today, Amrita?" Kalpana asked, her lips bent upwards in a gentle smile.

"I'm good. But I was worried about you. I hadn't heard from you in two weeks. That's the longest you've been away since we met."

Kalpana said nothing, slowly nodding her head. "You know you could have seen where I was if you wanted," she said in a few seconds.

"I know," Amrita paused. "But if you didn't want me to know, there must have been a reason."

Kalpana smiled at her pupil, a look of content washing over her face. "Let's take a walk," she said and started heading towards the thick trees away from the river. Amrita followed.

The two walked in silence for a few minutes. Amrita scrutinized her vicinity. Even though she lived in the forest, and had traveled to countless other forests, she couldn't recognize this particular one. The alignment of the trees was unfamiliar, even though the tall oak trees were similar to those in Amrita's home forest. Noticing Amrita's perplexed look, Kalpana said, "I've never brought you here before." Amrita looked back at Kalpana, hoping for more information.

"Today is an important day in your training. The magic you'll learn today, it's the last thing I have left to teach you," she said and paused. "Well, second-to-last, technically, but that's irrelevant for now. And there's an important place I have to show you afterward," Kalpana added.

Amrita thought about that. Last bit of training, some important place. What was Kalpana going to do? Kalpana was always clear about the purpose of their lessons-- every time, she started with a detailed overview of the skills and techniques they would learn that day. It was unusual for her to be so obscure. And a place to show? "Where are we going? I mean that important place you mentioned, what is it?" Amrita asked.

"Oh, it's just a place across the river," Kalpana casually replied. "But first, your training. Now this is something you will have to master in the next few months. Walk with me until we reach where we need to be."

Amrita complied, and the two walked for almost half an hour. The serene forest stretched on as dapples of light filtered through the foliage and created pools of moving light on the ground. Even though the forest looked mostly untouched by human activities-- there were no signs of recently cut trees and the wild grass grew in abundance-- Amrita noticed that the path they were taking looked previously walked upon as the growing grass and fallen leaves were stamped onto the ground to resemble a thin trail. In fact, there were similar faint trails criss-crossing the forest. Amrita yearned to know more about this forest. But before she could ask Kalpana, the trees parted away to reveal a clearing covered in lush, well tended grass. Kalpana stopped here. She opened her coat and dropped it below a tree trunk at the edge. Walking to the center of the clearing, she beckoned Amrita to stand in front of her.

"Today, I will teach you how to stop an attack," Kalpana said, her voice switching into a firm, focused tone she naturally caught when teaching.

Amrita nodded. She wasn't sure why she needed to learn to stop an attack, but this was the most aggressive thing she'd had to learn so far. "You go to that end and I'll be at the other. I'll throw some hurdles at you and you try your best to stop me," Kalpana instructed and retreated to the edge of the clearing. Amrita walked to the other end, the distance of the clearing spacing them apart.

Amrita also opened her coat and dropped it to the ground. She took a deep-breath in. If she was going to fight Kalpana, she would need all her strength, even though this was just practice. Kalpana's magic was effortlessly glorious— she performed the most complex spells with ease.

The next second, Amrita saw a blaze of fire emerge from Kalpana's palms and shoot towards her. Amrita wasn't sure what to do. Just as the fire reached her, she raised her palms in front and said, *"Jalashaya"* A water barrier formed in front— the fire crashed into it— a scorching sound emanated as the water transformed into a cloud of vapor. As she walked out of the cloud, Amrita's hair, face, and clothes were moist. She raised her eyebrows at Kalpana, asking for an explanation of what had just happened.

"That was not bad," Kalpana said. "But I want you to use your special power to stop me. Yes, you could stop an independent attack with what you just did. But with your powers, that seems like child's play. I wanted to see what your first reaction would be. But now you have to learn the new technique."

Amrita nodded. "First, you have to open your mind the same way you have every time you've used this kind of magic. Open your mind, but don't lose your own perspective. Then enter the opponent's mind. Can you do this much?"

"Yes, Kalpana. I can."

"Now, the next step is to feel the opponent's magic as your own. Understand— know— what is their next step? If they are about to launch fire, feel the flames in your hands. And stop it— like you are stopping your own thoughts, your own magic." Kalpana instructed.

"How will this be different from other times I've practiced this magic?" Amrita asked.

"Great question. The process is similar to every other time you've used magic. But since you are interfering with someone else's magic— and not just thoughts— it requires much more focus and energy."

Amrita sighed. This sounded difficult. "Are you ready to try now?" Kalpana asked.

"Yes, Let's," Amrita said and moved back to her position at the edge of the clearing. By now, the sun was higher up in the sky. The grass clearing was mostly washed in light, apart from the edges outlined by some tree shadows. More birds had come out and their voices reached the two women from different parts of the forest. Even though Amrita could not identify the birds, the jovial crescendo of voices felt as though the tiny creatures were beckoning them to come and play.

Amrita closed her eyes and focused on Kalpana, and the next second she could feel the energy of Kalpana's incredible magic. She felt Kalpana prepare to cast the spell of fire, she felt the energy of the flames in her own hands. And, in the final moment, when all the energy was built up inside her, and all that was left was for Kalpana to say the spell and release the flames, Amrita firmly said, like she was directing her own magic, "Stop!"

The next moment, she felt light— all the energy of the flames had vanished. Amrita opened her eyes. She was back to being herself. Looking across, she saw Kalpana had fallen onto the ground.

"Are you okay?" Amrita asked, rushing towards her teacher.

"Yes, I'm fine." Kalpana said, pulling herself up. "All the energy knocked me down for a second there, but I'm fine. Excellent work, Amrita."

Kalpana picked up her coat from the ground and put it on. "That's all for today. Let's go back now."

Amrita retrieved her coat from the other end and the two women began walking back.

"Now that you are twenty-one, and nearing the end of your training with me, there are some things I have to tell you." Kalpana started saying.

Amrita quizzically looked at Kalpana. Kalpana had never mentioned this before, about a big milestone coming at a certain point. "Okay," she said, hesitantly.

"Remember, when I first met you and explained to you about magic— how every person's magic is unique in some way, and your aptitude included the ability to reach into other's minds, experience their thoughts, and even change them?"

"Yes, of course I remember," Amrita replied, curious where Kalpana was going with those words.

"Well, there's something I didn't tell you back then." Kalpana paused for a moment. "You are the only one who can do that."

Amrita was silent. Why hadn't Kalpana told her this before? This sounded like too important of a detail to have forgotten. Kalpana must have deliberately kept this information from her. But why?

"I know this sounds confusing," Kalpana continued. "But I wanted to finish your training before telling you this. You are the Healer— a special magical role, part of the House of Justice. Only the Healer can do mind magic like you can." Kalpana explained.

Amrita didn't know what to say, but felt a rush of questions. Knowing her pupil well enough to predict her reaction, Kalpana continued, "I'm guessing that you might have a lot of questions, and we will eventually get to all of them. But for today, I only want you to remember the things I've told you. Now I have to show you something."

They had now reached the riverbank where they had first met that morning. The river was before them— its flowing water still casting the peaceful, soft music.

"What are you showing me?" Amrita asked, confused. There was nothing before them, only the continuing forest at the other side of the river. Maybe it was something to do with the plant species of the forest? But as she'd noticed earlier, these species were the same as the ones in the forest of her home.

Kalpana smiled gently, her eyes brimming with excitement. She pointed at the land across the river. Amrita watched Kalpana wave her hand and when she looked back across the river again, the trees were melting away—

slowly— to reveal a busy street full of people. Colorful houses with shops overlooked the street. Amrita saw people going about their business like nothing miraculous had happened.

Amrita looked at Kalpana in disbelief. "It's time for you to come back, Amrita." Kalpana said.

CHAPTER TWO

VINES

Twenty-six years ago

A festive joy permeated through the valley. Joyous, upbeat music burst from the small, wooden windows. Light blue flags, with a small sparrow at the center, flurried in the gentle spring breeze from where they were planted at the sides of doors and windows. As the people walked, they looked happier and more vigorous than usual, dressed in their best daura-suruwal and sari. Festivals were months away in the autumn, but the excitement that day was comparable to that of any festival. It was the inauguration day of the cabinet of ministers, carefully chosen by the parliament elected by the people.

Many citizens had already poured into Tundikhel— a vast ground designed for public occasions like this. Chairs were placed in meticulous rows— ornate wooden ones in the front for the parliament members and smaller metal chairs for the rest of the audience. A stage was set in the very front with twelve seats for the twelve newly elected ministers, who had not arrived yet. The metal bars enclosing Tundikhel were decorated with garlands of colorful spring flowers like azaleas, daisies and irises. Just below them, blossoms of lilies and tulips growing from the ground added more adornment. Light pink rose petals gently fell from the sky in a slow, steady pace— like snow— and vanished seconds after touching the ground. There were occasional chocolates that fell too, and children rushed to catch them, eagerly waiting for the next one and discussing if it would be bigger than the last one they had caught. To the children's relief, chocolates did not vanish after they were caught. The adults were huddled in groups, talking about the elected officials, discussing their personal approvals and disapprovals.

"I think the education minister will really improve the government school system. She's qualified and she's visionary," someone could be heard saying.

"I agree. But having vision and ideas does not equate to action. Does she have the grit to push through the system?" Someone else replied.

At the stage, a group of five musicians, each of them equipped with their unique instrument— a flute, madal, sarangi, piano and guitar— were playing traditional tunes to mark the occasion. Their sounds blended mellifluously to fill the open grounds with a sense of lightheartedness and optimism.

At noon, the president arrived, followed by the ministerial candidates. When the people saw them, they settled down in their chairs. Dressed in a simple, golden sari, the president, a heavy woman in her sixties, walked onto the stage. When she poised herself in front of the podium, ready to address the audience, the music stopped, as did the shower of flowers and chocolates.

"Namaste! Welcome to the inauguration ceremony of the cabinet of ministers," she said. A loud cheer emerged from the crowd.

"Today is an important day for our nation. Every new inauguration reminds us of the sacrifice our people have made to make today's democracy possible. It was only two decades ago that a war was raging in these very places. The struggle was difficult, but the people prevailed. More than the celebration of our new officials, today is a celebration of how valiantly our nation upholds the rule of the people. So every time that a new government is created, we must not forget to honor the sacrifices of those before us, and promise to protect this land for those who are coming." A solemn silence had fallen upon the crowd who was listening intently to the President's words.

"To begin the ceremony, I invite on stage— the Healer, Awadesh," she stopped for a moment and looked at the front row. She saw that the Healer's designated seat was empty. "Awadesh, are you here?" She said again.

At that moment, the metal frame of the main gate to Tundikhel, which had been locked for the ceremony, opened. A man walked in. He was dressed in a white daura-suruwal, and a thin black coat fell from his shoulders, all the way to the ground. Despite this salient entrance, he radiated a sense of calm energy. Nothing about him suggested the slightest superiority over those sitting. He was simple, but by no means ordinary.

He walked towards the stage through the narrow aisle between the chairs. Climbing up the steps of the platform, he stopped before the President. "Yes, madam President, I am here. I'm sorry for not coming earlier-- I guess I underestimated the time it takes to walk to Tundikhel from the city border," he said in a soft, firm voice.

"Excellent," the President said, smiling at the Healer. "Now that Awadesh is here, we can begin the ceremony. As you all know, all ministers were selected by the Prime

Minister, and have been approved by the Parliament. Now, the final approval remains— from the Healer." She paused for a moment, allowing some time for the audience to understand this important procedure.

Seconds later, she continued, "The Healer will look into the essence of each candidate and assess their ability to serve this nation. If the candidate is approved, the Healer will release golden flames into the sky. If not, he will release black flames. Let the process begin." She stepped off the podium and with a wave of her hand, pushed it to the end of the stage so that nothing obstructed the view of the elected ministers who had been listening to the President from their seats. Now, they shifted their gaze to face the audience. Even as they were excited for this new appointment-- smiling at the audience and waving occasionally-- a hint of nervousness lingered on each of their expressions.

The Healer walked over to the first minister, who promptly stood up. With a gentle smile, the Healer lifted his right hand in front of him, waiting for the minister to match it. The Healer could look into each person without touch, but this gesture symbolized mutual respect. Quickly, the first minister placed his hand against the Healer's palm.

The Healer, Awadesh, closed his eyes and everyone was silent– anticipating the result. The crowd's eyes stayed-- unmoving-- on Awadesh. Even children understood that something important was happening and stopped fidgeting.

The next minute was one of those occasions when someone gets to appreciate how long a minute can be. Everyone in the crowd felt like a long time had passed when the Healer opened his eyes and shot flames from his hands into the sky that burst in a brilliant, yellow glow. The crowd burst into applause. The minister who had been approved smiled and waved to the crowd, relief washing over his face. His appointment was final now-- he was officially a minister.

The ceremony for the next ten ministers passed similarly, and at the end of each, Awadesh released brilliant golden flames into the sky. As more ministers were approvers, conversations started amongst the audience, who began to talk about the qualities and prospects of the approved candidates again. When it was time for the final minister, he and the Healer placed their hands against each other, like the eleven ministers before him. The crowd was much less tense now, many were talking to each other, and they expected golden flames for the final minister as well.

But when Awadesh opened his eyes, no one saw the look of alarm in them. Flames rose from his hands, but burst in a dark, black color in the sky.

A gloomy shadow fell upon the crowd. With shocked expressions, people looked at each other, wondering what would happen next. But the constitution was clear— a person disapproved by the Healer could not become a minister. Never before had a Healer released black flames for a ministerial candidate, but it had happened for the first time with Kuruk Nayan.

It was that time in the morning when night hands over the reins to day. The chief commander of the day— the sun— was not out yet but preparations were underway as darkness began to slowly fade away and a subtle orange light in the horizon inked the first traces of the day's beginning. The air was cool and fresh— its touch to the face brought a sense of calm that could not be found after the day's hectic affairs had begun.

Almost all the people in the valley were still asleep. And alone, in the streets walked Awadesh, the Healer. Morning time before sunrise brought him the most peace-- it was a time when he could relax, without thousands of thoughts and energies crashing onto him from every direction. From his solitary home in the hills, Awadesh had transported himself just outside the valley's border. After that, he preferred to walk, relishing the day's calm beginnings.

As he walked past the houses overlooking the street, he felt a faint energy of the people still sleeping. Each person's energy felt like a small fire spark. The presence was strong enough— like a spark– to know it was there, but not strong enough to overwhelm him. Soon, he had passed through the houses to reach the town Center, Satdobato, from where seven roads diverged, each leading to a different place.

At the center of Satdobato was a small lotus pond. The majestic pink petals of the lotuses rose peacefully above the water. The flowers did not let their graceful presence be disturbed by anything— their calmness of the morning would persist through the day and spill into the night. Awadesh knew he could never achieve that level of calmness— his magic wasn't made for that— and perhaps that was why the lotuses struck him so much.

Awadesh took the first road to his left— a quiet path, lined with trees. There was an occasional house, but this path led away from the city and did not have the signs of settlements– residential homes or apartment buildings or business complexes– of the other paths. He wanted to continue walking on this serene path for longer, but after an hour, he arrived at this destination, stopping before a short, wooden gate.

Opening the gate, he walked inside to a large schoolground. At its right edge was a giant peepal tree, shading over a brick platform, the chautara, where he had spent so much time as a child and teenager. The main education buildings were some meters behind the chautara. Far into the end of the grounds, hidden behind trees, was the small wooden cottage where his Guruama lived. Her name was Kabita, but all her pupils called her Guruama. Awadesh intended to meet her.

Arriving at the front door, Awadesh knocked. As he waited, he scrutinized the garden which was his Guruama's passion project. Lilies, irises, roses, and tulips that Guruama had been planting when he had come two months ago had bloomed beautifully with spring's arrival. The aaru tree, at the edge of the compound, was heavy with ripe fruits, leaving only a few pink blossoms that had not ripened yet and appeared like delicate garnishes amidst the thick leaves and ripe fruits. Seconds later, a short woman in her late fifties opened the door. The moment she saw Awadesh, a wide smile brightened her face. Awadesh bent and touched her feet. The woman put her hands over his head for blessings. "Come in," she told him, walking inside.

They entered a small living room. The center of the floor was covered by a blue carpet, with a sofa set atop it. The windows were small but intricately carved wooden enclosures. As Awadesh stepped inside, the mud floor felt cool below his feet. The house was exactly as it had been when he was a child. As spells were invented and tested on building materials, new construction techniques had been invented— people now built homes with concrete, stone and even glass, which was the latest technology, rapidly increasing in popularity. But Guruama's home stayed the same. When he had suggested she shift to concrete a few years ago, she had said she would never abandon her mud home, where she felt connected to the Earth. Living in a concrete house, she said, would strain her and make her sick. She had told Awadesh that she believed her bond with the Earth, from the time she was a little girl— working in the fields with her parents, helping them with seasonal plantations and harvests— was what had helped stabilize her magic, eventually making her his Guruama.

"Let's sit," she said to Awadesh, pointing at the sofa.

He looked at her and said, "You first." She concurred, and picked the side facing the window, as the first morning rays began to spill in. Awadesh sat next to her.

"I heard about what happened yesterday," she said, referring to the inauguration. She knew why Awadesh had come and did not waste any time on small talk.

Awadesh said nothing. Pursing his lips, he looked down. His eyes fell on the edge of the carpet where geometric patterns of red and blue criss-crossed each other. His mind flashed back to the inauguration ceremony. Traversing through the minds of the candidates, he had seen hope, optimism and determination— more in some than others— to take the country forward. But with Kuruk, it had been different. There had been some good things— flashes of genuine bonds with people, visions of innovative development ideas— but everything was overshadowed by his ambition. The deeper he went, the stronger the darkness became— a maddening desire to get power above anything else. There was no sense of service to the nation or its people. No doubt, Kuruk was an intelligent man. But within seconds, Awadesh had known that such a man could not become minister– he was not suited for a public service role.

"What are you thinking about?" Guruama's voice brought him back to the present.

"I am worried about someone like Kuruk ascending to power. When I looked into him, there was just so much darkness. It frightened me. I don't understand how he got there," he said to Guruama, worry embedded in his eyes and the cadence of his voice.

"Well, not everyone has the ability to look into a person's true intent like you. Despite everything, Kuruk is a very intelligent man and has some charm. These mingled with some populist speeches and slogans, gave him the parliamentary seat," she said. "But that's why you're here, Awadesh. It's your gift to stop people like Kuruk from taking power. Shouldn't you be happy about that?"

Awadesh exhaled. Yes, he had stopped Kuruk. For now.

"But I've got a really bad feeling about that guy. I can't stop him every moment, in everything he does. And... I just don't think it's going to be good in the long term," he said, dejected, and unsure about what exactly he was afraid of.

Guruama smiled gently at her pupil. "You're right. You can't stop him every time. But Kuruk is an adult— he has to choose who he wants to be. Good or bad, he has to take responsibility for his actions. But if he chooses the evil path, and tries to do something that threatens the nation, you will be there to stop him. Just take solace in that for now."

Awadesh nodded. He had folded his right leg up on the sofa so that his face rested on his knee. As he thought about what Guruama had said, he hoped she was right.

"Now let's go outside. I will pick out some fresh aaru for you. You've always liked them," she said, getting up from the sofa.

Feeling a little more comforted, he followed her to the garden. Ever since he had first met her when he was five, Awadesh could always feel better with Guruama, the woman who had trained him for years and helped him harness his magic. At least for now, when he was with her, he could permit himself to cast his worries aside.

A small crowd had gathered in the grounds of Adarsha Madhyamik School. There were no classes since it was Saturday. In the small, rectangular playground overlooked by the school buildings, plastic chairs were placed in rows. It was a winter morning and the land was dry— dust released into the air as children, who had come with their parents, scurried around. The hundred chairs that had been arranged in a neat square formation were only half filled. The organizers— a group of fifteen men standing at the front— looked disappointedly at the turnout. Dressed in a warm red sweater and black pants, one of the men, with sharp eyes and a thin mustache, stood without a trace of worry. He looked at his wrist-watch and said, "We'll start in ten minutes."

"But the seats aren't full yet," one of the other men told him.

"We will start when we said we would. Not waiting for anybody. Those who had to come will have come, Dipesh," the man said.

"As you say, Kuruk," Dipesh replied. With a wave of his hand, Dipesh elongated a small wooden plaque and turned it into a low stage. From his bag, he took out a microphone.

Exactly at noon, Dipesh nervously walked onto the stage and said, "Namaskar everyone. Welcome to today's program. Without further delay, I want to invite today's chief speaker, Mr. Kuruk Nayan, onto the stage." He rushed off the stage and handed over the mike to Kuruk, who confidently walked into the stage.

"Namaskar brothers and sisters. Thank you for your presence in this very important event for me," he started. "As you all know, I was selected last year as the Home Minister, but was stopped by the Healer. Your presence today to listen to me speak means everything to me. Thank you." He paused for a moment. The crowd showed no reaction.

"But despite what happened last year, I am not willing to give up because I want to continue fighting for the future of our nation. Because our magical community still has a long way to go before things are equal. And I will not let anyone stop me from working towards that. It has been two decades since monarchy ended, since the people's government was established. But has this brought significant changes in people's lives? No— the schools in the villages don't have enough teachers or facilities. Drinking water, housing, food supply— those are the continued struggles of daily village life. Why should people of the villages continue to suffer? Is it fair that only the people in the cities get everything, while the citizens of the villages, who truly struggled to bring in people's government, remain untouched by development?" Kuruk's voice had now increased, his words flowing in a fiery tone. "No," he continued. "It is neither fair nor right. We have to change this and I am ready to fight to end this suffering, to bring true justice." He stopped and took a deep breath in, for effect. A silence had fallen over the crowd. While they were listening to Kuruk, it was hard to tell if they were convinced by those words.

"But they won't let me. Even when I was elected and ready to take office, the Healer stopped me. After all, who is the Healer working for? The nation? The people? Or Himself? You all know about the previous work I've done and work that my family has done for our nation. During the war to end monarchy, my father was jailed for a full year– a time of prolonged ordeal when he was kept in terrible conditions that I cannot even speak of the details now. But, he told me that he would take all that pain all over again for our nation. And I was raised with those values and convictions. So why did the Healer stop me from becoming a minister? Was it because he cared about the nation or was it because he felt threatened by me?"

"So, despite the events of last year, I am here to tell you all that I will continue to fight for our nation. We cannot let this inequality go on any longer. And to stop our nation from moving backward, I need your support. I know that the past year has been difficult for me, but despite that, I want to assure you that I am here for you all. Thank you again." With these words, Kuruk bowed and stepped off the stage. Slow claps emerged from the people, some looked at each other with doubtful gazes while others were nodding. Claps slowly increased but they were still hesitant, it would take time for the claps to mature into open, uninhibited applause.

That night, Kuruk lit a fire in the middle of the woods where his team was camping and sat next to it in the cold, winter night. His hands, freezing minutes ago, now felt warm and relaxed. Behind him, fifteen tents had been propped up. Oil lanterns had been enchanted to hover in the sky and cast a soft, yellow glow over the men as it mingled with the silvery glow of the half-moon. Some of Kuruk's men had left a few hours ago to for for a hike and to look at some local plants for dinner. Others had already fallen asleep after a long day's work.

Rubbing his hands, Dipesh— one of Kuruk's childhood friends and most trusted team members— hurried towards the fire and sat a few meters away from Kuruk. He impulsively put his hands above the fire.

The two men sat in silence for a few minutes. In the quiet forest, the only sound they heard was the wood cackling in the fire. "Nice speech today, Kuruk," Dipesh said some time later, his voice meek and kind.

"Yes, thanks." Kuruk replied dismissively.

"So what are we going to do next? After this month's tours are over?" Dipesh asked.

"Well," Kuruk paused for a moment. "I don't know. But we have to figure something out. Have to start some project in the villages. These village people are our voting base, Dipesh. We have to work consistently to build trust with them." Kuruk said.

"Elections are still over three years away. You've been working so hard for the past few months..." Dipesh trailed off, not daring to suggest that Kuruk take a break.

"Yes, we have to work hard-- we don't have a choice. Especially with what the Healer did in the spring. You know how much the magical community reveres the position of the Healer. What he did-- it was irreparable damage. If it was anyone else, I'm sure they'd have given up by now," Kuruk paused, a reflective tone cast over his face. "Anyways, if we start early, it will be easier when elections arrive." Kuruk calculated. "If people realize from early on that they can trust us, they will vote for us. But if we work hard, I think it is possible for us to be victorious again."

"I want nothing more than for you to be elected again," Dipesh said and was quiet for a few seconds. Then, he asked another question, "But even if you are elected, the Healer will still have the final say. How do you plan to stop him? With his kind of magic, you know that the Healer can stop hundreds of people attacking him at a time."

Kuruk glared at his friend for speaking so highly about the Healer. Dipesh winced, almost wishing he hadn't spoken about the Healer at all. But a moment later, Kuruk's expression softened. Dipesh was, nonetheless, right. "We have to figure out a way to get rid of him," Kuruk said in a cold tone.

Dipesh paused for some time."You don't mean, kill, do you?" Dipesh asked, nervous.

"Of course not. Even if I wanted to, I couldn't kill him. In that regard, you're right— he is too powerful. But ever since that day of the inauguration, I have been thinking about how I can put the Healer out of my way so I can become minister. I won't stop until I find a way, Dipesh," Kuruk said decisively. From his tone, Dipesh discerned that Kuruk did not want to discuss the subject anymore.

For the next hour, the two men sat silently next to each other, in the warmth of the fire. Every time the wood burned out, Kuruk added more from a nearby wooden pile and then shot flames at it from his palm so that the diminishing fire roared again. Every time Kuruk did that, Dipesh felt slightly guilty that he hadn't replenished the fire first. But Dipesh couldn't help but feel in awe of the glorious fire that Kuruk lit. Kuruk had always been talented this way— a nonchalant, simple hand movement from him created such dazzling flames. Dipesh was certain that if he'd lit the fire, it would have been feeble and small.

A few minutes after Kuruk had relit the fire for the fourth time, they heard voices. They were jubilant voices, carried in from a distance— Kuruk and Dipesh couldn't make out the exact words. Minutes later, they heard footsteps against the forest floor's foliage and the five men who had left for the hike returned.

"You've been gone for a while," Kuruk said to them. The five men walked by the fire and suddenly the quiet setting of moments ago resembled a boisterous picnic.

"Yeah, the path was very peaceful and the sunset was brilliant so we just kept on walking," Abhinav said. "We walked all the way to the top of the hill and sat there for some time."

"And Pritam found a new plant, which had some vegetables growing in between the vines, on the hill-top. We're roasting it in the fire and eating it today," Ritesh said.

Taking out an elongated, green vegetable from the bags, Pritam said, "It looks somewhat like a cucumber, but a little different I guess. Anyways, it'll be a welcome change after only eating rice, daal and spinach for a week. Do you want some Kuruk?" He offered.

"No, I'm fine for today. I'm feeling pretty tired so I will go to sleep," Kuruk said, standing up. "Maybe Dipesh will try some," he added, patting Dipesh on the back before walking away to his tent.

Dipesh looked at the other boys and felt a sharp desire to be away from the crowd. "I think I will also just go to sleep today. Good night boys," he said.

The voices of the other men receded as he walked back to his tent, which was at the very end. Passing Kuruk's tent, he saw a glow inside. So Kuruk hadn't slept yet. Dipesh wondered if he should go talk to Kuruk, but quickly dismissed the idea and walked to his own tent. It has been a long, hard day and he deserved some rest. Tomorrow, they would be traveling to a new village and he had lots of organizational duties. He entered his small tent and lit the lamp on his bedside table. He wondered if he should read for a bit-- the book he was reading was a riveting tale about an adventure to find a magical gem with healing powers amidst the mountains-- but he felt exhaustion take over his body. The moment his head touched the pillow, he fell asleep.

The next morning, the cold felt more intense than the previous day. Clouds covered the sky, forming a misty layer that shielded the sun rays from reaching below. Kuruk woke up, still feeling tired. The moment he stepped out of his tent, he heard commotion at a distance. He walked towards the sound. By the fireplace of last night, some of his men were gathered— arguing.

"What's going on?" Kuruk asked.

Hearing him, they stopped talking. Pritam spoke forth, "It looks like some of us have lost our magic."

"What do you mean lost your magic?" Kuruk asked, confounded.

"Well, when I woke up this morning, I decided to pack up my tent since we're going away today to a new location," Abhinav started to explain. "But when I tried to do the shrinking spell, it didn't work. None of the spells I tried worked. I panicked. When I came out, I found out that the same thing had happened to others too."

"We're trying to figure out what the hell happened," Ritesh said, flustered.

"So everyone has lost their magic?" Kuruk asked, a hint of panic in his voice.

"No, just the five of us— Pritam, Ritesh, Abhinav, Rupesh and me," Ghanashyam replied "That's why we've been worried sick. Why have the five of us been hand-picked to lose our magic?"

Kuruk began to think. He hadn't heard of any enchantment or advanced spell to take away someone' s magic. What would explain this? The men started discussing again— panic rising in their voices.

Kuruk thought about what connected the five. Had they done anything differently from the rest of the group? In the morning, they had all prepared together for his event, and all of the group members had been present at the school during the speech. After that, they cleaned up together and came back to their camping site. Yes— it struck him– these were the five men who had gone off on their own to hike yesterday.

"Stop," he said to their quarreling voices. "You five are the ones who went on that walk yesterday evening. Did you meet anyone on the path, or stop at a house for water, or eat something strange?"

"No," Pritam replied. "We didn't meet anyone. But there couldn't be a plant that could take away our magic, could there? If there were, wouldn't we have learned it in Magical Plants and Animals Systems class in school?"

"Well, these parts are new to us. We have to be exceptionally careful. Try to remember," Kuruk promptly said, convinced that the key to their conundrum was somehow connected to their hike yesterday.

"Now that I think about it, there was that cucumber-like plant," Abhinav hesitantly began.

"Yes! The one that you brought back yesterday. Were you five the only ones who ate it?" Kuruk asked.

The five who had consumed the plant nodded, looking at each other. Dipesh too was standing amongst them, his arms folded.

"Dipesh, did you eat it?" Kuruk asked, startling Dipesh.

"No, I went to bed before eating it," Dipesh said.

"And you have your magic?" Kuruk frantically asked.

Dipesh responded by shooting a quick jet of water from his palm.

"The plant could be it then," Kuruk said. "Do you have some left? Let me see it."

"Umm, I think we ate all of it," Rupesh said, softly.

"Then take me to the place you found it, now!" Kuruk commanded.

All men complied and quickly began walking towards the hilltop from yesterday. In the rush of the moment, no one remembered to enjoy the beautiful road overlooked by lush trees and intermittently peppered with purple and white wildflowers. As they neared the top of the hill, snow began to fall in gentle wisps. Soon they were at the top of the hill, which was open and windy, making for a splendid sight of the settlement below.

"Here's the plant!" Abhinav said, pointing at it.

The rest of the group rushed towards him. Kuruk saw that the plant looked exactly like a cucumber. The vines of the plant, in the absence of a sturdy supporting beam, had netted themselves on the grass, and the vegetables— long cucumber-like but thinner— popped up from between. The green vines were covered with a thin layer of freshly fallen snow, which diluted their bright green color. Kuruk bent and picked one.

If only there was someone familiar with the plant who could tell him about it. Kuruk looked around. A few hundred meters away, he saw a figure looking away from the hilltop at the settlement below. He approached it.

"Excuse me, can you help me please!" he said, beseechingly rushing towards the figure.

It was an old man, his face wrinkled with age, but there was a bright glow in his eyes. He turned to face Kuruk as he was approaching. "Yes, son. What is it?" He said in a gentle voice.

"Can you tell me what this plant does? My friends had eaten it and they seem to have—"

"Lost their magic?" The old man said, nonplussed. "Don't worry. That is the *Him Lahara* or Snow Vines, an extremely rare plant found in parts of the mountains and some hills. It takes away a person's magic for seventy-two hours. Their magic will be back then, once the plant's venom has been flushed out of their bloodstream."

Kuruk breathed a huge sigh of relief. "But if I were you, I'd throw away that plant. Even though magic will return in seventy-two hours, every usage of the plant slightly weakens a person's ability to do magic. They even say that excessive use of Him Lahara can completely rob magic from a person," the old man cautioned.

"Thank you, thank you so much," Kuruk said, relieved, and began to walk back to his friends. But as he walked, he did not throw away the plant, but clutched it tighter in his hands, as an idea took charge of his mind.

A young, fourteen-year old girl sat in a school office. She was wearing her school uniform— a plain white kurtha with a light purple border on the edges, and matching pants and shawl. She had short hair, which made her look younger than her age. She had never been to an office like this before— those of her school teachers were plain and simple with a desk, a chair, a cupboard or bookcase and a few additional seats for occasional guests. But this office had flowering vines which covered one of the inner walls. Spread throughout the room were multi-colored flowers in pots that infused the room with a sweet aroma. The chair, desk and cupboards were there, but mingled with the flowers, the furniture appeared to have shed their somber quality and absorbed the flora's vibrance. A large bookcase occupied another wall, filled with colorful book spines. She wondered whose room this was.

A few minutes later, a woman entered the room. She was wearing a plain blue sari. Her hair— composed of interlacing black and white strands— was tied in a bun. There were some wrinkles in her face, but they did not snatch away her youthful energy, but appeared, somehow, to enhance it.

"Thank you for coming here today Kalpana," she said to the young girl.

Kalpana simply smiled. "You must be wondering why you're here. I'll tell you about all that. My name is Kabita and I am a teacher," she said.

Kabita paused, in case the child wanted to say anything, but Kalpana stayed quiet. Kabita continued, "A month ago, I got a letter from your school principal with a list of students who were excelling in their classes, and asking me to observe them. I agreed. I get these letters every year, you'll know why in just a while. If you noticed, I was in some of your classes. I observed all students, looked at their academic record, and after thorough evaluation, I've decided that you were perfect for the job."

Kalpana looked back at Kabita, perplexed. "What job?" She softly asked.

"You must know about the Healer?" Kabita asked.

Kalpana had studied about the position of the Healer and its extraordinary powers of mind magic— a magic that allowed them to read others' minds and experience their thoughts, feelings, and essence. The Healer was also capable of changing thoughts, but that power was limited by the law to rare occasions. While she knew these facts, she had only seen the Healer once— when attending the inauguration two years ago with her parents. It was an event that had been permanently etched in the history books of the magical community. The Healer had shocked everyone by releasing black flames into the sky for one of the ministeres. Kalpana still vividly remembered that moment. As golden flames had been released one after another, the crowd had relaxed and eased into conversations. She too, sitting next to her friend, was discussing about what ministries they would handle if they became ministers. They had settled with the Education Ministry for Kalpana. Just then, the black flames had been released-- covering the sky in a smoky ink. A hush had fallen upon the crowds. Kalpana had been confused. She had only been told by her parents about the golden flames. "Yes, I've read about the position of the Healer in school books," she replied, thinking back to that day.

"Then you know that the Healer is not one person. The magical energy of the Healer transfers to a new body after a certain time. Awadesh will not be the Healer forever, and we must start preparing for the next Healer," Kabita firmly said.

Kalpana understood everything Kabita had said so far, but she couldn't fathom how she was related to it. "Now when a new baby is born as the Healer, their magic is incredibly unstable. Perhaps required by the job description since Healers have to perceive the world around them so intricately. But, as you know, unstable magic can be very destructive. If left that way, it will destroy the person with that magic," Kabita paused. She opened the drawer and took out a thick book, with a golden cover and yellowed pages. Kabita placed it on her desk and continued, "That's why the law has provisioned for a teacher who helps the Healer to learn to stabilize their magic, while enhancing their gift of mind magic. I was the teacher for the current Healer, Awadesh. And you, my dear, have been chosen to be the guru of the next Healer."

Kabita stopped, giving Kalpana time to absorb this. Kalpana carried a dazed look, having widened her brown eyes. She clearly needed this time.

Kalpana wondered about it. Could it be true? She— the trainer of the Healer— the teacher of the strongest magical practitioner and possibly the most important figure of the magical world? But Kalpana had never imagined herself to be chosen for a job as important as this. Yes, she liked studying and enjoyed it. But she was also shy and quiet-- hardly noticed by anyone. Thinking about her career, she had imagined that she would become a librarian one day-- a job that enabled her to mostly stay quiet and be lost amongst books. Imagining anything important, like during the conversation with her best friend about becoming the Education Minister, were just fun and games. She knew that, her friend knew that and they approached it with the same light-heartedness that they would a game. "But, why me?" She hesitantly asked.

Kabita smiled at her gently. "I wondered if you might ask that. Because Kalpana, your magic is the most stable I have seen in years. Trust me— I get letters to find the Healer's teacher every year. But I haven't seen anyone cast spells the way you do," Kabita paused for a moment and looked down at her desk, thinking of how to phrase everything she knew and believed about the young girl before her.

A few seconds later, she looked back at Kalpana and continued, " I could see that you've mastered the spells by practice, and your extraordinary effort is the foundation of your stable magic. You are genuinely interested in the spells, you go to the depth of each one in ways others don't, and that gives you an advantage in understanding magic, and helps make your magic fluid and inventive. You don't realize though, that you are also a natural. Despite all this, you never take magic for granted. And I know you never will. And to train the Healer, perhaps the most unstable magical energy, we need someone like you." Kabita paused and picked up the book she had taken out minutes ago. Extending her arm towards Kalpana, she said, "Please take this book." Kalpana got up from her seat and took the book, which felt heavy in her arms. This was the thickest book she had encountered. While she was excited to explore everything that the book contained, she also felt daunted.

"That's the first volume that will teach you how to train the Healer. You can take it with you and look through. Now, before anything else, I must ask you. Do you accept this job?" Kabita expectantly asked.

Kalpana wanted to say yes. It would be her honor to train the Healer. But was she really qualified for such an important job? The woman across from her certainly thought so. "So you really think I can do this?"

"Yes Kalpana," Kabita firmly said. "There can be no one better for the job. I will personally teach you moving on, and you have much time to learn. The next Healer isn't even born yet!" She added with a touch of levity.

Kalpana smiled. "Then yes, I accept the job."

Months passed by and Kalpana commenced with her learning. She had daily sessions with Kabita, who conscientiously taught her everything she needed to know. Kalpana had mastered many of the basic spells and was quickly moving up to intermediate spells. With Kabita, she felt an ease of learning that she had never experienced with anyone before, and she became grateful that she had been chosen for this job.

On one such training day, fifteen months after Kalpana had accepted her job, she was sitting outside in the chautara with Kabita for another training session. It was monsoon and rain was falling heavily from the sky. Kalpana loved rain and she had been the one to ask Kabita if they could train outside. Kabita had agreed and had enchanted the tree's leafy branches to form a shield over them so they wouldn't get drenched by the rainwater. Accompanied by the water's soft, falling sound in the background, Kalpana focused on what Kabita was saying.

"So far, you have studied spells that help you understand the Healer's magic and communicate with it. Starting today, you will learn magic that will enable you to directly interact with the Healer's magic. You should know that the spells you learn next will connect your magic and the Healer's magic in very powerful ways," Kabita paused. Kalpana nodded her head, excited about this next step.

"Today I will teach you a fundamental spell to help you stabilize the Healer's magic," Kabita continued. "Since the Healer's magic requires them to look into others' minds and consciousness, it is naturally designed to pick up these energies. When untrained, this power can cause a great deal of distress— the Healers may feel that they are hearing multiple voices and experiencing overwhelming feelings from all directions. You— as the Healer's teacher— can help them stabilize these voices by giving them a stable energy created from your magic."

Flipping through the yellow book of spells, Kabita stopped at a page and handed it to Kalpana. Kalpana saw that the page contained an image of a small circular energy which looked like light. Below it, in bold letters, was written, '*Sthayitwa ko mantra.*'

"Ok Kalpana, you should be standing up for this so that your posture is more flexible," the older woman said, standing up herself.

Kalpana stood up. Her teacher continued, "This is a very important spell. It allows you to channel your magic into a symbol that you can then insert into the Healer's body. This stable energy will be an anchor for the Healer to learn to control their own powers better. I will now teach you to conjure that symbol."

Kalpana nodded and took a deep breath in. This spell was unlike any other she had tried before. She felt a rush of apprehension and impulsively rubbed her palms against her kurtha. She was glad that it was raining-- the sound of the rain impinging on the ground and the cool feeling as some raindrops slipped through the shield and fell into her skin created a feeling of calmness.

"For this spell, you have to relax. You need to channel your most calm and stable energy to this symbol," Kabita said. "Start by closing your eyes."

Kalpana immediately did so.

"Take your mind to a memory when you felt calm. It must be a happy memory, but the most significant mood should be calmness," Kalpana heard Kabita instruct her.

Kalpana probed her memories. Immediately her mind went back to the river by the forest in the valley's border. Her entire family had gone there for a picnic, five years ago. While her cousins played hide-and-seek and chor-police in the forest grounds, she had been drawn to the flowing motion of the water's current— powerful but serene. Sitting down by the riverbank, she had dipped her feet in the river and watched it flow through, meandering around the big rocks stationed at the river's path. When Kabita asked her to think of a calm memory, her mind went back to how the river felt on her feet and the vision of its waves.

"Did you think of it?" Kabita's voice asked. Kalpana slowly nodded. "Good," Kabita said. "Now I need you to connect with your inner magical energy. Let the calmness seep into the strength of your magic."

Kalpana took a deep breath in and brought her palms in front of her chest. Slightly separated, her palms hovered there for some moments as worked on the spell. "When you're ready, procure a small symbol of your magical energy," Kabita gave a final instruction. Kalpana focused more within herself, connecting her magic and her memory, and felt a warm energy rise inside her that happened every time she cast a spell. But this warmth was different. Every other time, the warmth had been a tiny flicker that came in and flashed away in a second, but this warmth stayed— as though washing over every cell in her body. This warmth was calm and soothing, as though, somehow it was created by heat and water coming together.

"You've done it, Kalpana. You can open your eyes now," she heard Kabita's triumphant voice.

Opening her eyes, Kalpana saw that a small ball of water was hovering between her palms. The water inside was moving in small, uniform waves, creating a soft sound. She smiled.

"Excellent work! You've figured out how to do this. But you must practice the spell regularly, okay. You can let the water go for now," Kabita said.

Kalpana relaxed her hands and brought them down. The ball of water vanished.

"Now, take a five-minute break and we'll move on to the next spell." Kabita said.

"Before that, I have a question," Kalpana quickly chimed in. "In the book, there was a ball of light in the diagram for the mantra. But I created water."

Understanding Kalpana's question before she had fully framed it, Kabita said, "The symbol is unique to every person who casts the mantra, based on their personal magic."

"So what was yours?" Kalpana asked.

Kabita brought her two palms in front of her and closed her eyes. Seconds later, there was a radiant, red flower between her hands. "It's a red rhododendron," Kalpana said, recognizing it from the images she had seen in her books about flora and fauna within the magical community.

"Yes, it was my favorite flower growing up. You don't find it here, but it was prominent in the hills where I was born," Kabita said.

Just then, the wooden gate of the school opened and a young boy ran towards them. "Guruama!" He screamed when he saw Kabita standing in the chautara. Kabita's flower vanished and she looked back to see who was calling her. The young boy ran towards her at full speed. He was breathless, and soaking wet from the rain.

"What's the matter?" Kabita asked, a hint of worry in her voice upon seeing someone coming to speak to her in such a rush.

"Awadesh," the boy said, in between breaths. "Awadesh has vanished, he's nowhere to be found."

CHAPTER THREE

ENCOUNTER

Present Day

Amrita looked at the settlement that had appeared in awe. "How…" she started but couldn't finish, too dazed to say anything.

"There's a protection spell that prevents anyone on the outside from looking in. I temporarily disabled it for us," Kalpana filled in.

"But… it's so big," Amrita said, still looking at the town in wonder.

"Are you ready to go in?" Kalpana asked.

"Yes," Amrita firmly said.

Kalpana directed her hands towards the river and raised some water. She threw her hands forward in a quick motion— casting a spell from her palms. The next second, a shimmering bridge of ice connected the two riverbanks. "There used to be a wooden bridge here, but it collapsed some time ago. Let's go now," Kalpana said and stepped on the bridge. Amrita followed, walking carefully on the ice.

When they had crossed, Kalpana cast another spell so that the bridge dissolved into water and fell back into the river. Then, she reinstated the protective boundary. They were now ready to venture into the town that had opened up before them.

Kalpana and Amrita walked on the central street, houses on both sides. Most houses had shops of different types in their ground floors facing the street— grocery stores, clothing shops and small, local eateries. In the clothing shops, packaged items– from saris to kurtha-suruwals to dresses– were springing out of shelves as the saleswomen showed them to customers, and in a corner, clothes that had not been bought had been enchanted to fold themselves to be put away. In the tea shops, the shopkeeper had arranged for the snacks— samosas and pakaudas and neemkis— to pop in and out of the frying karai without his supervision. In the kirana pasal, the owner spoke to different customers and took their orders, while the rice, daal, chana and chiura were being self-measured from the sacs.

Voices bargaining for lower prices spilled into the street and mingled with the chatter of pedestrians and occasionally, a bicycle's chirping bell. The street was bustling with people who emerged from different shops with huge bags. Amrita's attention fell onto a woman walking with three full bags of vegetables hovering beside her and three small children, as tall as the vegetable bags, skipping behind. As the children laughed and pushed, one of the little boys collided with a vegetable bag and potatoes and cauliflowers tumbled into the street. The woman looked back at the mess, annoyed and pulled the boy's ear before repacking her vegetables. Amrita smiled and looked away.

The walk after that was more somber. As she watched the people and the houses, she perceived a lively energy of the people around her. But unlike at home, the energy now was sprinkled with the touch of magic. Every person's magical energy was unique and left imprints of its own. But with Kalpana's training, Amrita had learned to separate these energies, and they did not coalesce into one indistinguishable, overwhelming energy that threatened to drive her to insanity. Amrita rejoiced that she could navigate this magical world so precisely.

After walking the path for half an hour, the two women reached a junction of seven streets. Kalpana stopped walking and told Amrita, "This is Satdobato. It's the center of the valley. Each road here leads to a different town."

Amrita looked around the busy junction. Vehicles and people emerged from one of the roads and vanished into another. But Amrita's eyes were captivated by the small pond of lotuses in the center. She rushed towards the pond. Kalpana followed.

Amrita stopped in front of the pond, which was enclosed by a thick brick wall. She gently traced her fingers on the wall's top surface. A dozen, radiant lotuses had bloomed beautifully— the rested calmly in the water. The placid lotus pond— unaffected by its surroundings— soothed the street's hectic energy.

"What happened Amrita?" Kalpana asked from behind her.

"This lotus pond. When I was small, I kept seeing a pond like this in my dream. I was so sure I had been to a place with this pond. But every time I asked Buwa, he'd say we'd never gone somewhere like that, that I must have dreamt it all," Amrita said, looking back at Kalpana.

"Well, you were right. You left the valley when you were four, so there must have been times when you came here with your family. If you live in any part of the valley, it is impossible to miss this lotus pond. But, as you know, your parents couldn't talk to you about the valley after you had left," Kalpana said. Linking her arm through Amrita's, she added, "If you're ready, shall we go?"

"Okay," Amrita softly said. Following one of the streets, Kalpana led Amrita through a quiet street, lined by trees. It was a residential area, there were small houses next to each other. Some had big compounds and were hidden away behind a lush vegetation while others were little cottages with a small flower garden in front.

Some minutes later, Kalpana stopped in front of a small cottage. It had a ground floor, and one room at the top adjoined to a kausi. The walls were painted a light yellow on the outside. The top floor had a sloping roof of brown tiles that gave the house a rustic feel. The wooden windows were large and exquisitely carved, although Amrita couldn't make out the exact design from that far away. In the front was a small flower garden, but there weren't many flowers there now. "Are we meeting someone inside?" Amrita asked.

"No. Amrita, this was the house you were born in. You lived here, until you were four, before your family had to move. I thought you'd like it to be the first place you see when you're back," Kalpana said.

Amrita glanced back at the small cottage. As she scrutinized the garden, she remembered a time when it was blooming with flowers– tulips, roses, irises, poinsettias, when the grass was a lush green and her parents would be running behind her in a game of catch. Growing up, she had always felt that she could recall memories of being in such a garden. She knew, deep inside, that those memories were real, but unable to associate them with a specific place, she had convinced herself that they were a dream too, just like the lotus pond. As she grew older and became occupied with the increasing demands of school work, those memories became figments that she barely visited. Now it was clear where they had originiated.

Would her parents still be alive if they had been living here? Would Ama have had that accident if they'd never left the magical world?

"Your parents had bought this house just before you were born," Kalpana said.

Amrita's mind flashed through moments she might have had with them here— birthdays and special parties, ordinary days of school and homework and even fights. It would have been a simple, fulfilling life.

"Thank you," she whispered to Kalpana.

Six years ago

Amrita remembered the first time she had met Kalpana as though it had just happened— like she could extend her arm and grasp it, even though it was six years ago. She had been in class ten. The year's first rains had washed the city as spring faded away and monsoon began. For Amrita, the day had been ordinary— one class after the other with teachers pushing them to study more and practice more for the board exams. When it was time to go home, at four pm, the sky had just cleared after a full day of rain and a subtle sunlight fell onto the ground through the parted clouds. Amrita walked towards the school's back gate. Other students were huddled in groups, laughing and talking as they prepared to walk home while the younger children waited for their parents to come and pick them up. But Amrita preferred to walk home alone. While her classmates were not mean to her— she still felt that they didn't completely understand her.

The end of school that day was like every other, except when she walked into the street, she noticed a woman sitting on the bench in the sidewalk. She was wearing a pair of jeans, a light-pink t-shirt and a sky-blue jean jacket that matched her pants. Her hair was neatly combed and tied behind. Amrita didn't know her, but she felt, almost certainly, that the woman stood up when she saw her and had been waiting for her. Impulsively, Amrita crossed the street and walked towards the woman.

Standing in front of the woman, Amrita didn't know what to say. Should she just introduce—

"You are Amrita?" The woman asked first, expectantly raising her eyebrows.

"Yes," Amrita replied.

"I'm Kalpana. I need to talk to you. Can we go somewhere?" she asked.

"I'm going home. We could talk there if you want," Amrita suggested. It took her a moment to realize that she had offered to take home a complete stranger. But for inexplicable reasons, that felt like the right thing to do.

"Sounds perfect, lead the way," Kalpana said, picking up a purple backpack from the bench.

The two of them walked quietly in the street, which had been changed by the touch of rain. The cemented pavement was damp, and small puddles had formed. There were less cars and people than usual. Water droplets, stuck on tree leaves and branches, were being coaxed to the ground by gravity. The air was cool and the people that passed by looked calmer than the usual, frantic pedestrians of a sunny day, as though they had absorbed some tranquility from the falling rain.

After walking for fifteen minutes, Amrita opened a black gate and entered. She pulled out keys from her pocket and opened the door. "Come inside," she told Kalpana. " I used to live here with my father."

Kalpana followed her in, scrutinizing the flat. There was a large living room, a bedroom that looked mostly unoccupied and a third room— with a study table, bookshelf, a cupboard and a small bed by the window. Photographs of natural sceneries—hills, forests, waterfalls, oceans, rivers— probably retrieved from old calendars, were pasted on the walls.

"Your room?" Kalpana asked.

Amrita nodded.

"Let's sit here and talk," Kalpana said, entering the room.

Amrita sat on her study chair, and Kalpana sat on the bed. Amrita felt like she was sitting with an old friend— like somehow, everything was just how it was supposed to be— even though she had never met Kalpana before.

"I'm Kalpana, I've told you that, and I have something very important to tell you," Kalpana paused. She took a deep breath in, "I'm not sure how exactly to tell you this, but have you always felt like there was something different about you?"

"Like somehow I didn't belong here? All the time. When Buwa was with me, it was better. Every time I felt very sad, I talked to him. But these past few months, with him gone— they've just been horrible," Amrita said. That was more than she had ever spoken about her father after his death four months ago. Every time a school friend, a teacher, or the neighbor— Deepa aunty who had offered any help she needed after her father's death— tried to talk to her, Amrita felt her words get stuck in her throat. In the months after his demise-- she had felt frustrated by the paradox of her reality-- she was upset that she didn't have anybody to talk to about her situation, but everytime someone approached her, offering comfort and a listening ear, she felt that she could not talk. But with Kalpana, she felt she could say everything about herself and it would be just the right thing to do.

Kalpana pursed her lips and listened to Amrita, a compassionate look in her brown eyes. "I think there's a reason you feel out of place here. Because Amrita, you were born in a magical community. A complex political history created a situation where you had to be moved to a non-magical place. But I am here to help you learn magic. Amrita, I am your teacher," Kalpana said.

For a moment, Amrita said nothing. Then, her eyes brightened and she smiled— earnest, uninhibited. "Can you show me?" She softly asked Kalpana.

Kalpana nodded and brought her right hand in front. She whispered something that Amrita couldn't quite make out, and the next minute, there was a small fire glowing on her palm.

Amrita watched in awe. She didn't know what to say. A few seconds later, Kalpana extinguished the fire and said, "So I was thinking of starting your training tomorrow. In the magical world, everyone has a unique power— some are good with construction, while others may make good artists. Your specialty is of a very sensitive nature and it'll probably be best for you to live away from people— like in a sanctuary. I was thinking of somewhere in the nearby woods? I'll show you what I have tomorrow and then we can decide. Amrita, I also want you to complete your education here so you'll continue going to school. And in the evenings and mornings, I will train you. How does that sound for now?"

That was a lot of information at once so Amrita simply nodded. "Great!" Kalpana excitedly said. "I will come to pick you up at nine am tomorrow. So, I'll go for now." Kalpana stood up from the bed and walked out of the room. In the hallway, before she could leave, Amrita said, "Wait. I have a question." Kalpana turned around to face her. Amrita continued, "You said that I can do magic. How didn't I know that, all these years? That's a pretty big thing right? One would certainly know something so significant about oneself?"

"Yes," Kalpana said. "If a person has magic, they'd definitely know it. That's why when you left, we gave you this," Kalpana came near Amrita and pulled the small, silver locket she was wearing from beneath her shirt. "The locket helps neutralize your powers to some extent."

Amrita looked down at the locket. Her father had told her that it was an important heirloom, and that she must wear it at all times. The one time she had taken it off— for fifteen minutes when it got stuck in her woolen sweater— her father had behaved as though some catastrophe had occurred and had made her promise never to take it off her neck again. She now understood that he was worried that her magic would show.

"I understand," Amrita said.

"Okay, I'll see you tomorrow then," Kalpana said and left.

That night, as Amrita went to bed, all her thoughts were about what magic would be like. Her mind, which was always haunted by anxious thoughts, felt alive with the joy of a new beginning today. After she had lost her father, her mind had felt as though it was a thin layer of film that anxiety could penetrate with the tiniest prick and completely take over. But meeting Kalpana, she felt hopeful. That night, Amrita slept uninterrupted by nightmares in a long time.

Amrita woke up early the next morning, and made breakfast for herself— fapar ko roti, fried potatoes and milk— and dressed in a simple yellow kurtha. Exactly at nine, Kalpana drove to her front gate and Amrita hopped into the car.

"How are you today, Amrita?" Kalpana asked.

"I'm feeling good, actually." she replied.

"I'm glad. And you can call me Kalpana," she said, making it clear for Amrita so that she didn't have to spend any time awkwardly trying to avoid calling her name.

Kalpana began driving. The car was small, perfect for a small family. Amrita wondered if Kalpana had a family, and who all were in it. While Kalpana seemed to know everything about Amrita's personal history, she realized that she knew nothing about the older woman's life. She began observing the car for any hints. The car was meticulously clean and the decoration was minimal, except for a sticker of a flowing river on the dashboard. The seats had soft, aquamarine carpets layering them.

Kalpana navigated the busy streets of the city and soon they had caught the forest route— much freer and emptier than city roads. Looking out, Amrita relished the cool air hitting her face through the window. After an hour of driving, Kalpana stopped the car. "We have to walk a little from here," she said, stepping out.

The two of them walked through the forest together. Amrita had never traveled to this part of the forest even though-- she realized now-- it was not very far away from where she had lived all these years. Amrita liked forests-- she would've enjoyed a hike or a picnic here with her father, but he had never shown an initiative to organize such an activity. Amrita could understand why to an extent-- having been uprooted from his home and his community, perhaps he had been too disenchanted by this unfamiliar place. And no matter how much he loved her, perhaps the feeling that she was the reason why he'd had to leave his entire life behind gnawed at him.

After almost an hour of walking, Kalpana abruptly stopped and said, "I've cast a protective spell around the house so that no one can get inside but you and me. Now, remember this point. From here a circle forms that surrounds the house," Kalpana instructed.

Amrita was perplexed. She only saw trees in front of her— identical to the rest of the forest. But she decided to wait for Kalpana to tell her what she meant.

"Okay, Amrita, take a step forward," Kalpana said.

As Amrita moved a step forward, she felt something cool wash her face and body. When she opened her eyes the next second, there no longer were the trees— but a a small wooden cottage overlooking a flower garden. A smile lit up her face.

"So what do you think?" Kalpana asked, nudging her.

"Kalpana, it's—" But she couldn't find the words, and she rushed towards the cottage to examine her new home.

It was a winter evening and the sun had set, infusing the sky with a subtle, orange glow. Amrita's winter break had started the day before, and she had come down to the city to buy some vegetables. Over a year had passed since she had first met Kalpana. She was in class eleven now. The break was a welcome reprieve. Her ability to perceive the thoughts of those around her was getting stronger everyday, and she hadn't fully learned to control them. At school, too, she would have to spend so much of her energy subduing the voices of her classmates and teachers that her magic picked up. Sometimes, they became too much. Staying home for a month would be good for her, she expected. Without too many intrusions— which always came when people were around her— she would get to practice techniques she had learned from Kalpana in peace.

The sidewalk was busy that evening as people hurried back to their homes to avoid the cold. In the main street, many cars passed by, possibly the people were returning home from work. While walking, Amrita felt fragile as thoughts of strangers around her entered her mind. Using Kalpana's training, she tried to stop them— the moment she detected a new thought she wrapped it in a shield of her magic and released it. Invisible, it then left her mind, no longer bothering her.

At that moment, she detected a new thought. Its energy was different from the others. She released the thought she had been working with, and just as her magic touched the new thought, a strange, dark feeling spilled into her mind. Amrita stopped— taken aback. As the thought took over her mind, she grappled with a dreary, dismal feeling. It became more powerful, and she felt her own thoughts and emotions slowly vanish— being replaced by a strenuous, evil emotion. More thoughts rushed in and each felt like a capsule hiding darkness that spilled open the moment it entered her mind—completely enveloping her.

Then, the voices began— first, one, then two, then many— starting out as low whispers, getting louder.

"The murder must happen today."

Amrita began to panic, her heart racing. "Stop," she said aloud. But that didn't stop the relentless voices. She focused on her magic, trying to create a shield, but it was too late.

The thought had spread too much— she couldn't contain it.

She looked around, trying to locate the source of these voices. But there were too many people— people rushing past her, vehicles driving by, shopkeepers and customers talking fast at each other.

The voices got louder. "Stop, stop, stop," she said in desperation.

Then, the voices coalesced into one. For a second, it was quieter. Then, she heard her own voice say—"The murder must happen today."

Amrita screamed.

Taking deep breaths in, she put her hand over her heart, and felt it beating rapidly. But it was of no help. The voice repeated.

She felt all her strength leave her body. People walking on the streets stopped to look at her. She fell to the ground.

"Take her to the hospital," she heard someone say before passing out.

After passing out on the street the day before, she had woken up in a hospital bed a few hours later. "It seems like you had a panic attack," the doctor had said. Now, Amrita looked out of the window, rapidly tapping her feet as she waited. At the wall clock, the time was one minute past nine. Kalpana should be here any minute, she thought.

Amrita saw Kalpana pass through the magical barrier and walk towards the front door. She rushed out of her study room and down the stairs. She waited behind the front door, which opened a few seconds later and Kalpana entered. Amrita immediately grabbed Kalpana's hand and took her to the living room and sat her down on the sofa across from her. Sunlight fell through the window on

Kalpana's black hair and blue jacket.

"What's the matter Amrita?" Kalpana was worried to see Amrita so anxious.

Amrita was quiet.

Then, suddenly, she started sobbing. She didn't speak, quietly wiping away the tears as they fell. Minutes passed and Amrita kept sobbing, unable to say anything. "I can't do this," she whispered, finally.

Then, the tears came more fiercely— as though somehow saying those words out loud had crushed an invisible barrier that had held back the tears. Kalpana had never seen Amrita like this. She moved closer to her pupil and held her, softly rubbing her arm with one hand.

"It's okay Amrita. I'm here. We can fix this together, we'll find a way," she softly said, trying to soothe her.

Amrita did not stop crying. She buried her face in Kalpana's jacket. "These voices— Kalpana— it's starting to become too much. Every time I go out— to school, the street— they come. I can't focus. I try to do everything you've taught me— I try separating them, defining them— I use all my magical strength, but it's too much," she said in between sobs.

"I know it's hard. But we'll fix it. Please just trust me. Try to be calm for now, okay?" Kalpana said. Hearing Kalpana's comforting voice helped Amrita somewhat to assuage her fears. Amrita took deep breaths to calm herself. A few minutes later, she had stopped crying, but she was still shaking.

"Okay, now tell me, what has been the hardest?" Kalpana gently asked.

"Too many voices. I can't control them. Sometimes there's a dark vision of the world, a warped perspective that my magic picks up. And suddenly— I feel like I'm not me.

Somehow, as though, those frightening thoughts are mine. And when multiple voices combine, I feel like everything inside me has collapsed," Amrita said, holding tightly onto Kalpana's hands.

"I know, Amrita, it's hard. That's the price of magic as powerful as yours, it picks up the energies and thoughts of those around you with such precision," Kalpana said, concurring with the struggles of her pupil. "And that's why we've been learning to filter these voices so that you control your magic and not the other way around," Kalpana explained.

"Yes, I know. But it's not working. Why have this magic if it's only going to break me?" Amrita insisted, moving from the couch to the floor, sitting below Kalpana— looking up desperately at her teacher.

Kalpana sighed. "It's difficult, I know. Mastering these voices— it takes time. But you can't give up now, you can't throw away this gift you have."

Amrita felt a rush of anger, she dropped Kalpana's hands and stood up. "Just because your magic is perfect doesn't mean we can all do it," she snapped. "Besides, you don't have the type of magic I do— you said that yourself— so how could you understand how difficult it is for me? I'm trying to tell you that it's driving me crazy, but you're not even trying to take my side!"

Kalpana looked at her, alarmed, and said nothing.

"So what do you want, Amrita? Just for me to give you back the locket? Just like that, you're going to give up?" she said a few seconds later.

Amrita, still upset, said, "Yes! That way, I can live in peace. Kalpana, I fainted in the middle of the street yesterday," she pleaded. "And what has training with you done for me? It's been eighteen months, and I feel more volatile than I ever did in my life. I thought magic would change things for the better, but it hasn't!"

Amrita began to cry again— partly because of all the pain she felt and partly because of all the things she had said to Kalpana. Despite her struggle, she knew that the horrible things she had said about Kalpana— her teacher, her friend— were not true. That, from the moment she had first met Kalpana, she had felt understood and seen for who she was for the first time in her life. But the hopelessness she felt about her magic somehow coaxed the most horrid words from somewhere— she couldn't even believe that she could think like that about Kalpana in her heart.

"I'm sorry," she whispered the next second, looking back at Kalpana.

Kalpana walked over to where Amrita was sitting on the floor, gently pulled her up and took her to the couch.

"I didn't know you passed out on the street. I'm so sorry that happened," she said. "I know these past few weeks have been extremely challenging," she added, looking at Amrita with a gentle gaze, "But I know you can do this, Amrita. In my heart, I know you will master this. But today, I can't let you give up, not until I've taught you to master your full potential. Then, knowing everything about your magic, if you decide that you don't want to use it, I will support you. But promise to try a little more now?"

Amrita took a deep breath in. She nodded.

Kalpana stood up and opened her scarf and jacket. "Today I will cast a spell that will help you stabilize your magic more, okay? I was planning to wait a few more weeks before doing this, but I think now is appropriate," she explained.

"Okay," Amrita said, feeling slightly better.

Kalpana closed her eyes and brought her hands in front of her. A few seconds later, there was a small ball of water between her palms. Tiny waves moved inside the ball, creating a soft, peaceful sound. Kalpana levitated the water closer to Amrita, until it was directly in front of Amrita's chest.

Then, slowly, Kalpana pushed the water through Amrita's body. The moment the water was inside her body, Amrita felt a surge of calming energy— all her worries and anxieties vanished— all the dark voices she'd accumulated in the past week were subdued.

"That will help you stabilize your magic. It will be easier for you to channel your magic and control the voices. I'll leave it there until your own magic becomes stable enough," Kalpana informed her.

Amrita looked at her teacher with grateful eyes. "So are we going to start another lesson now?"

"Yes, we'll do that sometime today. But first I think we should go and get some ice-cream," Kalpana said, getting up from the couch.

Amrita smiled, and got up too, and the two of them walked out the door.

CHAPTER FOUR

CYCLE

Twenty-four years ago

For a moment, Kabita did not believe the young boy. How could Awadesh vanish? He must have left town or stayed away. He was the Healer, after all. How could anyone do anything to him?

"I'm sure that's just a misunderstanding," she told the boy, whose name was Raju.

"No Guruama. The staff of the House of Justice checked his home thoroughly, there was no sign of him," Raju said.

Standing next to Kabita in the chautara, Kalpana just listened. She was not sure what to say or do, and she kept quiet, believing that the older woman could handle the situation.

"Maybe he's gone out of town," Kabita suggested.

"I don't know everything Guruama, but Awadesh was supposed to come to the court yesterday, but did not. The Supreme Court staff wants to talk to you, so they sent me to call you," Raju said.

Awadesh would never skip a session at the Supreme Court if he had promised to come. A hint of panic entered her heart, but she blocked it. No, there must have been some other explanation. But she would have to go find out.

Turning to Kalpana, she said, "We'll continue this lesson again sometime. I have to go to the court for now."

Opening up her umbrella, Kabita rushed towards the garage. She entered her little blue car. Soon, she was driving out of the school's wooden gate and on the path towards Satdobato. Rain accompanied her— droplets fell on her car's roof in a rhythmic beat. The wipers in the car's front glass were moving rapidly to push away the heavy flow of water. Besides the beats of rain, the street was quiet. The lush trees lining the roads were drenched and this enhanced their green color, making their presence more marked than other days. The road was mostly empty and Kabita was glad— she did not want to navigate through heavy traffic on a day she was already anxious.

In fifteen minutes, she arrived at Satdobato, which was slightly busier than the road before. Intermittently, cars emerged from one of the seven paths and seconds later, vanished into another. The lotus pond was quiet and majestic— like always.

Kabita steered her car, taking the road to the capital's administrative complex. Unlike the forested path before, this road started with buildings on both sides. They were all administration complexes of various ministries. Only the outermost structures were visible from the main road, but the government buildings stretched much deeper to encompass working spaces for the central employees of all twelve ministries. At the end of the main road, after a drive of ten minutes was the Supreme Court— a tall, regal building distinguished by its blue tower-like facade.

Kabita drove in through the Supreme Court's gates and parked her car at the edge of the front yard. She grabbed her umbrella and got out, walking in quick steps towards the tall wooden door entrance. Below her knees, a cool sensation seeped through her sari as the falling rain hit it. At the front door, the staff of the Supreme Court were waiting and shot questions at her the moment they saw her.

"Do you know where the Healer is?"

"Did Awadesh leave you a message?"

"We can't find him in his house. Do you know where he might have gone?"

"Shhh," Kabita said, overwhelmed.

"Sorry," the chief security officer of the House of Justice spoke up. "Why don't you take a seat and we can figure this out," she directed Kabita to the end of the hall. Walking past the main courtroom, which was empty, Kabita entered the small living room at the end of the passage. This was the Supreme Court's meeting room for judges and was currently half full with people— the core staff members of the Supreme Court including the judges and the Chief Justice. They rose to greet her. Kabita sat down next to the Chief Justice. From the somber look on all their faces, Kabita inferred that they must have been discussing something very serious, possibly related to Awadesh's apparent disappearance.

"Guruama," the Chief Justice, who was a stern man in his late sixties, began, "As you know, the Healer severs as the chair of the House of Justice and his presence is mandatory in all Supreme Court hearings. The case to be discussed yesterday was a very serious murder case which had been filed for the third time in the Supreme Court, since the victims were unsatisfied with the verdict of the District Court and High Court. In such a case, the Healer's presence is even more important to guide us in the right direction. With his abilities, he can detect any lie or attempts to tamper with the evidence. I had made it very clear to Awadesh that he must come and he had assured me that he would. But he didn't arrive at all— we waited the entire day."

Kabita did not know what to say. If Awadesh had promised to come to court, there was nothing she could think of that would stop him. She could no longer push away her worries which were clasping her heart.

"I can't think of a reason why he wouldn't come," Kabita meekly said to the Chief Justice, feeling helpless.

"Exactly," said the chief security officer, who had been leaning against the door frame. Walking into the room, she kneeled before Kabita and explained, "That's why we went with a search party to his house. But it was empty. Everything seemed to be in order— the bed was made, the utensils arranged. And, his desk was perfectly organized. We know how Awadesh likes to work at his desk— with all his books scattered. But this was as though he had not lived there for a while."

Kabita's fear intensified. Where could Awadesh have gone? "He hasn't told me anything."

"That's strange too. He always discusses any important job details with you, doesn't he?" The chief security officer asked.

Kabita nodded. She was not sure what to say.

"So to help us find him, we've called you Guruama," the Chief Justice said, sipping tea from his cup. "You were The Healer's teacher and your magic is connected to him. We were hoping you could use your magic to locate him."

"Yes!" Kabita immediately said, wondering why she had not thought of this herself first. "I can do that."

The room fell quiet and looked at Kabita in anticipation. Kabita closed her eyes and brought her hands before her. Seconds later, there was a small, glorious red rhododendron floating between her palms. She brought the flower before her face and softly blew on it, releasing it into the air.

"This flower is connected to Awadesh and his magic. I have directed it to take us to him," Kabita said, feeling a little more reassured.

For a few seconds, the flower floated in the air— all expectant eyes on it— the room silent. Kabita waited for it to start moving, providing them all with a trail to follow towards Awadesh.

But the flower did not move. Instead, it disintegrated into pieces and fell on the floor.

"No," Kabita whispered, gripped with terror. "This can't be." Everyone in the room looked at her, stunned. A fearful silence fell on the room. Kabita fell to the floor and began to cry.

Far away from the Supreme Court, at the other end of the valley and deep into the woods, Awadesh woke up. It was dark all around him. He felt a hard surface on his back. Where was this? Awadesh pulled himself up. Across him, at the top of the wall was a small window frame— barred by metal rods intersecting to form perfect squares. Gentle light fell from the window into the room, and it was the only light source into wherever this was.

To his right, long metal bars were extending from the ceiling to the floor, their round rods silhouetted in the minimal light. He rushed towards the bars. Wrapping his hands around two of the metal rods, he shook them. But they were rigid. Why was he behind bars? He examined the room. Apart from the bed, he distinguished the shape of a small desk and chair at the opposite end. This felt like a prison. But why—

"You're awake," a soft voice from the other side of the bar said. Making out the shape in the feeble light, he saw a small, lean man. He squinted to recognize the face.

"Dipesh," he whispered, and his mind flashed back to the events of the day before.

It had been an overcast morning— the skies were streaked with the gray clouds of monsoon. Awadesh had to be in the Supreme Court exactly at noon, and in the morning, he decided to read documents related to the case. It was still early and he was eating breakfast. Just as he took his first bite into his apple, there was a knock on his front door. He hadn't been expecting anyone.

He was surprised to find Dipesh standing there. He and Dipesh had attended the same school, and Dipesh was a few years younger. Even though Awadesh would be busy taking lessons of the Healer with Guruama, he still saw other children in the regular classes and in the playground during breaks. But he had never interacted much with them, and had few acquaintances from his time in school. He remembered that Dipesh had been a small boy, who was often left forlorn in the playground when he first joined the school, so Awadesh had made friends with him. They would often sit at the edge of the small pond in their school grounds, trying to spot the fish. After a while, Dipesh made some friends, and Awadesh became completely occupied by his Healer training.

"Namaste Awadesh dai, may I come in?" Dipesh asked.

"Yes," Awadesh replied, holding the door open. He was perplexed. He hadn't spoken to Dipesh in years so why had he suddenly appeared? Awadesh noticed that Dipesh was carrying a wooden basket. It was covered in a blue cloth.

"How come you've come to see me?" Awadesh asked, surprise carried in his tone.

"It's just that I was visiting Guruama this morning and she had made some sel-roti. She was looking for someone to deliver it to you, since she knows how much you like them. And I volunteered," Dipesh said, placing the basket on the table. "And I thought it would be nice to get away from the city and take a hike here. It's so much more peaceful up here."

Awadesh smiled slightly at Dipesh and removed the blue cloth. Freshly made golden sel-roti filled the basket to its rim. "Thank you for bringing these Dipesh."

"It seems like I came here at the right time," Dipesh said, pointing at Awadesh's breakfast.

"Yes," Awadesh said, pulled out a roti from the basket and put it on his plate. "Why don't you also eat one?" Awadesh added, retrieving a plate for Dipesh.

"No, no," Dipesh immediately said. "I mean, I just ate some before coming here. But I will have an apple if that's okay," he added.

"Okay," Awadesh said, handing an apple, from where he stored them in the kitchen counter, to Dipesh. The two men sat at opposite ends of the dining table.

Awadesh took a bite of the sel-roti. It was delicious like every other time— balanced to be crisp and soft, the sweetness blending perfectly with the flour and the spices like cinnamon and cardamom. But why did it also have a subtle, bitter aftertaste? I must be imagining it, Awadesh thought to himself and finished the roti. After all, a sel-roti could not be bitter.

The two men spoke for a few minutes, asking general questions about their life and family. "You have a really nice home here," Dipesh said, admiring the room.

"Thanks. Do you want to see the rest of the house?" Awadesh asked, getting up from his chair.

"Yes," Dipesh eagerly said.

Awadesh first showed the living room, which was simple— a sofa set and table with a flower vase in the center. There were two stalks of lilies inside. The wall consisted of two paintings— one of the snowy mountain range and another of the riverbank. The next room was Awadesh's study room. It was much livelier than the room before— the walls were filled with bookshelves and his study table facing the window was strewn with books, papers, documents.

There was a small table at the side with a knitting set— balls of colorful yarn kept in a box, and an unfinished red scarf. Just as Dipesh was about to ask Awadesh about it, Awadesh stumbled— leaning against his desk. Some of his books fell on the floor.

"Are you okay?" Dipesh asked.

"Yes. But strangely, I feel faint."

Awadesh pushed himself up with support from his desk. But the feeling did not subside. He felt a strange, dull buzz in his mind. He had woken up only two hours ago, but felt drowsy again. Pulling out his chair and sat down, and placed his head on the desk. At that moment, more voices of men emerged from the front door. Who was coming into his house? Seconds later, six men entered the room.

"Good job Dipesh," a stern, deep voice said. "Now clean up everything like we were never here and take him," the voice commanded.

Soon, books were flying across the room as multiple voices cast spells to sort them back into the bookshelf. The man who had commanded them was now standing directly behind Awadesh's chair. But before Awadesh could see the fact of who had spoken, he had passed out.

"What is this Dipesh?" Awadesh asked from behind the bars, back in the prison.

Dipesh remained silent.

Awadesh sighed. He brought his hands in front and said, "*Kholastra*" But nothing happened. "*Kholastra*," he said again. But again, nothing happened.

"That's not going to work," he heard another voice say. It was the same deep voice he had heard yesterday before passing out.

Awadesh gripped tightly on two of the bars. "Who are you?" He said.

A figure walked towards him and a few steps later was standing directly before. Awadesh gasped in recognition.

"Kuruk," he softly said.

"Yes, it's me." Kuruk took out a small vial filled with green liquid and showed it to Awadesh. "You can't do magic anymore. I poisoned you to take your magic away," he revealed.

"What is that?" Awadesh asked.

"It's a concentrated juice from *Him Lahara*. Do you know what that does?" He paused, glaring at Awadesh. "It takes away a person's magic," Kuruk said, his voice infected with condescension.

For a moment, Awadesh did not say anything— there was a stunned look on his face. Standing next to Kuruk, Dipesh nervously watched the two men. A tense silence filled the room. Then, Awadesh began to laugh— softly at first, then louder.

Kuruk frowned. "Why are you laughing? I just said I took away your magic and have made you my prisoner," he lashed out.

Awadesh pursed his lips. Yes, why had he laughed?

He knew his magic was gone. He knew, at that moment, he was powerless against Kuruk.

Yet, there was something about this situation that was so... predictably pathetic. Did Kuruk really believe— as he held that vial— that poisoning a man would bring him happiness? But knowing what he did about Kuruk, how could Awadesh have expected anything different. "Nothing," he said.

"Now that you are out of my way, there won't be anyone stopping me from becoming the minister next year," Kuruk said, a content tone in his voice. "And soon, I can become the Prime Minister," he said.

"Enjoy your prison," he dismissively said to Awadesh as he prepared to leave. "Dipesh here will be your guard," he added, placing his hand on Dipesh's back. "Let him know if you need anything."

Kuruk left the room. Only Awadesh and Dipesh remained— in complete silence.

"I've set up a desk for you over there," Dipesh meekly said a few seconds later. "You know, with books you might like and a knitting set. You might want to drink water, you've been out for over a day." With a quick motion of his hands, Dipesh lit a lamp by the desk— illuminating a stack of books, a jug of water, balls of wool and some stationary.

Awadesh said nothing, only stared at Dipesh. "I am really sorry for what I did Awadesh dai," Dipesh said, trembling.

Awadesh did not respond. He walked over to the desk and opened one of the books. Examining the titles, he said, wryly, "Why all this?"

"It's bad enough that you have to stay a prisoner. I thought you at least deserve to have a little bit of what keeps you happy," Dipesh said.

"And that argument convinced Kuruk?" Awadesh incredulously said.

"No, I just said you might be less trouble if you had something to keep you busy," Dipesh replied.

Awadesh picked up the water jug and took a few gulps.

"If you need anything, let me know..." Dipesh offered from the other side.

Ignoring him, Awadesh walked back to the bed and lay down, looking up at the lifeless, black ceiling.

Twenty-one years ago

Hari boarded a tempo. It was nine-thirty am. The tempo was almost full— only one or two seats left— in the morning's office rush hour. Inside the tempo, there were three other men— all dressed in crisp, white daura-suruwal and blue coats just like him, and five women in a blue sari with a yellow border. These were the standard uniforms for government officials. The people were quiet, and soft, melodious classical music played from the vehicle's radio. Sounds of moving engines and car honks came in from the road outside.

A woman across from Hari was eating a samosa while two other passengers had their faces hidden behind the daily newspaper. Hari looked up. The ceiling above each seat contained four buttons— tea, coffee, samosa, newspaper. Hari pressed on the tea button and chose black tea with sugar and milk. It had been a busy morning and he hadn't had time for tea. Seconds later, a small square enclosure opened from the ceiling and a cup of tea hovered out. Hari grabbed the cup and took a sip.

Soon, they arrived at Satdobato. The driver steered the three-wheeled tempo towards the administrative complex.

At the entrance, all passengers got off. Hari took out his identity card from his pocket and showed it to the guard before being allowed admittance.

The road inside was smoothly paved— the pedestrian sidewalk was wide and lined with shrubs and flowers. It was the morning reporting time so Hari saw many employees hurrying to their offices, just like him. Hari walked past identical concrete buildings— each labeled at the very top with the ministry it housed— for ten minutes before finally arriving at the one that read: Krishi Mantralaya— Ministry of Agriculture. He entered through the wooden front door and arrived at a hallway. This was the main building and many officials had their offices here. But Hari's was further behind in the wooden cottages, which had been constructed later to accommodate more workers as the ministry's work expanded. He exited through the back door and arrived at a large green lawn. The path to the cottages was at the edge of the lawn.

At the lawn's center, his friend Anubhav, the head of the Agricultural Chemicals Approval department, was bent over a marigold plant. There were five others with him. Hari stopped to watch. One of the men, who Hari supposed must be the creator of the chemical being tested, poured some liquid onto the marigold plant's soil. The entire group waited.

Soon, the marigold plant began to grow rapidly. Within seconds, the plant was as tall as the men. The creator of the chemical looked happily at his friends. Anubhav, his arms folded, watched intently, without a reaction.

But the plant did not stop growing. It grew and grew until it became as tall as the building. The pot shattered, startling Anubhav, who fell to the ground. The flower's roots invaded the lawn. The marigold's petals hovered in the sky like a giant umbrella. The creator's happy expression transitioned into a panicked one. This— clearly— was not what he had hoped for.

Anubhav pointed his palms at the marigold plant and emitted a green light. It stopped growing and burst into tiny pieces— flowers fell from the sky in a splendid orange glow, some reached Hari, gently falling onto him. Hari smiled, surmising that this chemical would definitely not be approved, and started walking to his office.

Inside the wooden cottage, Hari's office was the first to the right. He entered the room. Resting his briefcase on his desk, he opened the blue curtains first. Warm sunlight spilled in.

As he sat down on his chair, ready to open some files, Hari heard a knock on the door. "Come in," he said.

The door creaked open and a group of farmers, wearing the standard green fatmer's attire, were standing at the door. "Namaskar sir," they hesitantly said and walked in. Hari beckoned them to take a seat.

"How can I help you?" Hari asked.

"Sir, we are the same farmers who came here a week ago, to ask about the arrival of fertilizers," one of them said.

"Yes, of course I remember," Hari replied, thinking back to their interaction a week ago when he had promised that the fertilizers would be delivered by the end of the week.

"Well sir, nothing has happened yet," another man added, fiddling with the lace of his green daura-suruwal, which was faded. Hari noticed that his fingers were cracked— a testament to his hard work in the field. He continued, "We traveled a long distance and the only reason we had to come was for our livelihood. Without the fertilizers, our crops cannot grow properly."

"Until last year, everything happened so promptly," a woman said. "It wasn't perfect— the fertilizers and subsidies were not enough for everyone— but at least they came. But this year, I don't know what has happened..." she trailed off, despair ringing in her voice.

Hari did not know what to say. It was already shameful for the ministry that the fertilizers were not sent out in the first place. It was made worse by his promises last week that he'd get it done. He felt a pang of guilt.

"I understand," Hari started. "The very day you came last week, I enquired into why the paperwork was not sent, filled them out myself and forwarded it to my supervisor's office. I don't understand why it hasn't been sent yet."

"Khai, sir, we don't know what's going on. But you have to help us. We don't have any other person to rely on," the woman said.

"I will talk to my boss again today. There have been many new appointments in the past year, ever since Mr. Kuruk Nayan took office as the Agriculture Minister. I'm sure it's just the transition causing some problems," Hari said. "Thank you so much for coming all the way here to see me."

The farmers were quiet for a few moments. "Okay then, sir, we will go for today. We have to start making our way back to the village," one of them said. The group began to get up.

"Wait," Hari said. "Why don't you eat some snacks and tea before you leave?"

The group reluctantly looked at each other.

"Please, I insist," Hari said. He tapped on the mirror on his desk and sent out an order for five glasses of tea and ten samosas to the canteen. The food arrived minutes later and Hari's guests looked slightly happier after the snacks.

When they left, Hari walked out of his office and headed to see Rajan— his immediate boss, who had been transferred as the new supervisor of his department four months ago. Just as Hari raised his arm to knock, the door opened and Rajan walked out, talking to another man wearing a shiny black suit.

"Thank you so much sir, for helping us out on such short notice," the other man said to Rajan.

"Of course. If anything comes up, please don't hesitate to ask," Rajan said, grinning.

The other man shook hands with Rajan and left. "Oh, Hari-ji. Come in, come in," Rajan said, having seen Hari waiting at the door.

Hari entered the room and for a moment felt disoriented. His old boss of ten years, Paribesh, had retired five months ago and Rajan had been nominated by the minister to take over. Even though Hari had come to the office after Rajan had moved in, he had not fully accustomed himself to the new decor. With Paribesh in charge, the office had been simple, graceful, accessible. There had been a small desk, a few wooden chairs for other employees during meetings, a file cabinet neatly organized with a desk next to it with files that were most pertinent to the current projects. But Rajan had filled the office with so many new objects— a bigger mahogany desk, a new sofa set, an expanded cupboard. Paintings and photographs were scattered across the wall— some of temples and mountains, others of cities and fancy hotels— without a cohesive theme, as though haphazardly slapped together to show off the price value. Hari felt that it was too gaudy, but kept that evaluation to himself.

Rajan beckoned Hari to sit on the chair across from him.

"So, Hari. What brings you to my office?" Rajan asked.

"Last week, sir, I sent a file to your office for the approval of fertilizers and transportation subsidies for the year?"

"Did you?" Rajan asked, walking over to his cupboard and retrieving a stack of files. He flipped through multiple files before finally coming to the one Hari meant.

"Ahh, yes. It seems like you did send it," Rajan said.

"Sir, it is time sensitive and needs your approval as soon as possible," Hari informed his boss.

"Okay. I will approve it and forward it soon," Rajan said, closing the file and putting it aside. "Anything else Hari?"

"No. It's just that the fertilizers are already more than two months late. This delay has severely disrupted the farmers' production. I don't think waiting any more is prudent," he asserted.

"Hari, I understand. I have been very busy in the past week. As you know, our new minister has different priorities than the last one, so I could not get to this earlier," Rajan explained.

"Sir, if the Agricultural Ministry's top priority does not include the farmers— no matter who the minister is— I don't know what it should be," Hari said.

"Of course," Rajan said, somewhat brought to his senses. "I will forward the files you've sent today itself."

"Thank you Sir," Hari said, getting up from his seat. He left Rajan's office and went back to his own.

Sitting on his desk, he opened a file and began to read. It was a report about the previous year's grain production. Hari, along with two others, would have to make a presentation later that week with recommendations for improvement based on the data.

Two hours later, there was a knock on the door. When it opened, his friend Anubhav entered into the room. Smiling,

Hari said to him, "It seems like you had an interesting morning."

"Yeah," Anubhav said with a deep sigh. "There were almost ten chemicals to test today. Only two were approved."

"I saw the marigold disaster on my way to my office," Hari told his friend.

Anubhav laughed, remembering the incident. "Yes, it seemed like that chemical was too concentrated. The producer has promised to reapply next month with revisions. Anyway, I came to ask if you want to get lunch together?"

"Yes," Hari said, closing the file he was reading. As he was heading out the door, a frantic voice, from Hari's mirror on the desk, filled the room.

"Hari, Hari!" He heard his wife's voice.

Hari rushed back to the desk. "Yes, Bimala, I am here. Are you okay?" He asked.

"The baby— it's coming. Sita is taking me to the hospital— you come here directly okay!" Hari saw a flash of her face before it vanished.

He felt a rush of blood in his body. "I have to go!" he said, and picked up his briefcase.

"Yes, hurry," Anubhav said.

"Okay, Anubhav. We'll do lunch some other time. I'm going to go find a taxi to take me to the hospital," Hari said, rushing out the door.

"Wait, here—" Anibhav took out a set of keys from his pocket and flung them at Hari, "Take my car. It'll be faster that way."

Hari grabbed the keys. "Thank you," he said and ran out of the office.

Within five minutes he was out on the main road. It was not rush hour so Hari reached the hospital within fifteen minutes. He ran to the maternity department's emergency room. In one of the beds, he saw his wife laying down.

"Take deep breaths, Bimala," Sita, Bimala's best friend, was saying to her. "Look! Hari is also here now," she added as he came through the door.

"What happened?" Hari asked.

"My water broke about an hour ago and the contractions have started," Bimala informed him.

"Have you seen anyone?" Hari asked her, looking around in the emergency room.

"No, we got here only minutes before you. Someone should be here any second," Sita said.

Soon, a nurse came to enquire and noted Bimala's vitals. "Let's move her to the delivery waiting room. Doctors can see her there. It seems like she's almost ready," the nurse said.

Hari and Sita held Bimala's hands and helped her move. As they waited, contractions— small and large— came and went. Both of Bimala's companions tried to soothe her. Doctors came to examine her every half hour.

"It's time," the doctor said in two hours and asked for the bed to be taken to the delivery room. A group of nurses whisked away the bed while Hari and Sita were asked to wait outside.

Minutes passed by while Hari and Sita waited— sometimes pacing the hall, sometimes sitting down, other times trying to read a book. There were moments when Hari felt that the silence and waiting stretched on forever. Yet, at times, the waiting also felt peaceful, filled with a subtle assurance that in some time— very soon— he would be a father.

Finally, a nurse came out. "Congratulations! You have a new daughter!" She informed Hari.

Hari smiled, enraptured in joy. Sita, standing next to him, was smiling too. "Congratulations," she said to Hari.

Another nurse came out, and holding the door open, said, "You can see her now." Hari and Sita walked in.

Inside the room, Hari's eyes fell on the small blue bundle in Bimala's arms. He felt a light mysterious flood of joy in his heart. Inching closer to Bimala, he saw the delicate face of the baby for the first time. Two tiny, bright eyes looked back at him.

"Meet our daughter, Amrita," Bimala softly said.

Hari smiled. "Hi Amrita," he said. "It is so nice to meet you."

Far away from the hospital, deep in the woods, Awadesh felt his heart flutter. *Him Lahara*'s poison had weakened him after four years of use. But at that moment, he felt like a vital, powerful energy had entered his body. His pain faded away. Awadesh stood up from his bed. He felt a light breeze come in from the window and completely engulf him. He closed his eyes and suddenly his mind was transported to a hospital room, to a new born baby.

Awadesh opened his eyes. "She's here," he softly said to himself, "The New Healer."

Eighteen years ago

Moonlight spilled into the room— casting a mild illumination over the dark cell. His back pressed against the wall, Awadesh sat alone in his bed, looking out of the tiny window which framed the full moon.

"Three years, two hundred and seventy days," he thought to himself. Ever since the night of the new Healer's birth, he had kept count of each day that passed. Awadesh felt himself becoming weaker every moment. The poison of *Him Lahara* had been injected too deeply into his body. "It is time to tell Guruama," he thought.

He was not sure what time it was but his captors had eaten dinner. Dipesh came and slid a plate of roti and cauliflower through the bars for Awadesh.

Awadesh stood up from his bed and walked to the prison bars. With a wave of his hand, he cast a sleeping spell over Dipesh, who fell on the ground.

Directing his hands at the prison door, Awadesh said, "*Kholastra.*" The metal bars swung open. He walked out. Further away, there were two more guards— who met the same fate as Dipesh. Then, Awadesh stepped into the night.

Cool air washed his face. He pulled his coat tighter around his shoulders and took a deep breath in— filled his lungs with the open air.

He began to walk away from the prison and into the forest. It was the first time in years that he was using magic and he wanted to be away from the place where he had been imprisoned.

In the moon's silvery glow, Awadesh could discern the shape of trees as he passed through them. Dipesh did let him come outdoors for a few hours every day, but then, his perspective would be of a captive— the forest would be close to him, but he could not freely become a part of it. But today, he was free, if only for a short time.

Awadesh walked in silence for half an hour, relishing every moment of the air touching his face, every rustle of the leaves as he stepped through the forest floor. Then— he stopped. Raising his hands, he cast a protective spell around himself. He wanted to do this alone, without anyone's interference.

Awadesh closed his eyes and focused on Kabita and her little house. Immediately, he saw a vision of his Guruama, sitting in a sofa in her small living room, reading a book. When he felt his entire energy exist in that room with her, he said, "*Yatrayam.*" He felt as though a strong wind gushed in and carried him away— then everything became still. Awadesh opened his eyes and saw his teacher in front of him. She looked up from her book, squinting.

The next second, a wave of alarm washed her face. She put aside her book and stood up, walking closer to Awadesh.

"Awadesh," she softly whispered when he was directly in front of her, relief in her eyes. His face, she saw, had become lean. He had a beard. His hands were cold and dry. She felt as though he had lost a vital energy— as though somehow, someone had reached inside him and put out the candle of his soul. But this— him alive— was so much better than the worst image that had been rooted in her mind since the red rhododendron had disintegrated in the courtroom— of his death.

"What happened?" She asked.

Awadesh directed her to the chair and beckoned her to sit and sat down himself.

"Kuruk poisoned me with *Him Lahara* and kept me captive," he said.

Anger washed over Kabita's face. She felt an ache in her heart— as though someone had wrenched it out and was squeezing it. How could she have let this happen to Awadesh— she thought— even though she knew this was beyond her control. She started to cry.

"It's okay Guruama. It is not your fault."

"Wait," she said, suddenly. "But you are here today. That must mean—"

"Yes," Awadesh said. "The new Healer has been born. I came here to tell you that."

Kabita was quiet— absorbing the significance of this. "How long?" She asked seconds later.

"Three years," Awadesh said.

"Why didn't you come earlier?" Kabita asked, looking at Awadesh with sorrowful eyes.

Awadesh looked down at the floor, quiet for some time. "I wanted to," he then said, looking back at his teacher. "But I did not have my own magic. The poison has weakened me— taken away my ability to do magic. You know that the only reason I could come today is because the Healer's magic is connected to an unpoisoned life of the new Healer and me, so it allows me to do some magic. I did not want to use her magic anymore than I absolutely had to. You know the Healer's magic is not meant to be used that way."

"Yes," Kabita said. "But why now?"

"Because my body is starting to feel too weak. Soon I won't be able to do any magic despite this connection. I had to tell you before that. Besides, even if I had come earlier, I would be of no use to you. My body was already too weak to wield magic regularly."

Kabita looked at her pupil with understanding eyes. "But don't say that— that you would be of no use. You are much more than just your powers as the Healer."

Awadesh smiled gently.

"But I have been hearing rumors that Kuruk may become Prime Minister soon. Even as a minister, he's caused so much damage. How do we stop him?" She added.

Awadesh sighed. "If he is elected by the people and the parliament, there is nothing we can do. I don't have my powers of the Healer anymore," he despairingly said. "But she can— one day. And soon, Kuruk will realize that keeping me imprisoned will not be enough. He will come for her and she is too young to defend herself." Looking pleadingly at Guruama's eyes, he continued, "Take her away. Far away from all this. Let her have a childhood unmarred by dirty politics. She deserves that much."

Kabita said nothing, looking at Awadesh. She smiled slightly at how unexpected— how ironic everything was. From the first day she had started training Kalpana six years ago, she had always imagined that welcoming the new Healer would be a joyous occasion. Instead, Awadesh was pleading to have her taken away like a fugitive.

"I already lost you. I will ensure that the new Healer is safe. Tell me, who is she?" Kabita said, determined.

"Her name is Amrita," Awadesh said. "Daughter of Hari and Bimala. You must know Bimala— she went to your school— was an art student?"

Kabita smiled. "Yes, I remember her," she said. "I will talk to her very soon."

Awadesh nodded. The teacher and pupil were quiet for some time.

"But what about you?" Kabita asked.

"I..." Awadesh started but trailed off, uncertain about what to say. "I will go back to my cell. Kuruk should have no suspicions about the new Healer."

"Yes, but Kuruk does not know how the Healer's magic works. You could leave prison, you could choose to live outside. Even though you don't have magic, we can protect you," Kabita said, feeling hopeful.

A thoughtful look shadowed Awadesh's face. Could he really be free? In the hours, days, months, years he had spent in the prison— looking out through the small window-- at birds that flashed by or falling raindrops or the glorious full moon or the limited frame of shapeshifting clouds— he had wondered. What if he could be free? What if he could escape all this? But even after hours of rumination, his thoughts always came back to one answer— no. Even if he left now, he could not do his job as the Healer. And to ensure that Amrita had a chance to escape and grow to her full potential, he would have to make this sacrifice.

"While Kuruk is still focused on me, you have to get Amrita to safety. Besides, I don't expect to live for too long now," he said.

"No!" Kabita said immediately. "Don't say things like that!" Suddenly— to hear her pupil speak about death so casually— Kabita's heart shuddered, her eyes filled with tears. "You can't die, Awadesh!"

But she knew he was right. The vibrant color of his face, the glow in his eyes– had faded. His body was too frail— the poison had penetrated too deep.

Awadesh looked at the pain in his Guruama's eyes and tears filled his own. He had never admitted his mortality to someone else before— it had just been a hazy, mysterious idea in his mind. But now, saying it out loud, had thrust the hazy idea into the concrete frame of reality. He could no longer escape it.

"Don't worry Guruama. Perhaps this was how my life was fated to be. But we have hope again-- now that Amrita is here," he said to her. Kabita smiled slightly.

He raised his head and straightened his posture. "It's time for me to go back to the prison," he said to Kabita.

She took a deep breath in. "Go," she said, softly. In her heart, she knew that this was the last time she would see him.

Awadesh walked away from the sofa. He closed his eyes— waved his hand— said the spell.

Then, he was gone.

Kalpana walked into Kabita's office and found her mentor bent over the desk. The office was like it had always been— the walls were covered in flowering vines, the bookshelf was full of colorful titles and the potted plants were spaced out across the room. But now, the flower had lost vigor— as though they were holding onto their last breath before withering away.

"You called me so urgently, is everything okay?" Kalpana asked, walking over to where the older woman stood.

At the desk was a silver locket shaped like a triangle. It was split open and contained a reddish-green liquid.

"Kalpana, it is time for you to meet your student," Kabita started, and she explained everything from Awadesh's visit the day before.

"So she'll have to be taken away?" Kalpana asked, raising her eyebrows, struggling to grapple with the revelation.

"Yes, it will be safer for her that way. But, you will have to bring her back one day," Kabita said. "As you know, the untrained Healer's magic can be very unstable," she continued, pointing at the locket. "So, to protect her, I have created this. It can be worn as a necklace and will neutralize her powers."

"What is it made of?" Kalpana asked.

"It is a concoction of naturally calming herbs and I have cast a series of stabilizing spells. Together, they will prevent Amrita's magic from taking over her. It can't protect her completely— but it will strongly diminish its effects." Kabita then closed the locket and sealed it. "Let's go now," she said, heading out the door.

Kalpana followed Kabita and the two of them got inside her little blue car and drove away. She hadn't ever imagined meeting her pupil like this. What would it be like when she met her? Would she feel a special connection? Kalpana's heart beat rapidly, and she frantically tapped her leg as she sat in the car– the anxious energy was too intense at that moment.

After half an hour, they entered a quiet, residential area. Kabita stopped the car in front of a small cottage overlooking a tiny, square garden. Kabita got out of the car and signaled to Kalpana to follow. Kalpana glanced at the flowers of the garden— there were so many different types, colors, sizes– but they were all a blur as they rushed towards the front gate.

Seconds later, a man in his late thirties opened the door. He was wearing a white daura-suruwal and blue coat— the government uniform. Kalpana looked at her wrist watch and saw it was nine am. He was probably getting ready for work.

"Hari?" Kabita asked the man.

"Yes," he said. "Can I help you?"

"I am here to talk to you about your daughter, Amrita?" Kabita said.

Hari frowned for a moment. Then, he held the door open and said, "Please come in." He led them to the living room.

Some minutes later, a woman entered the room, holding the hands of a little girl. When Kalpana looked at that child, her heart stopped.

The girl was tiny and wore a blue dress with white spots. Her light brown hair was short and tied in a small pony-tail. She was smiling as she looked up at her mother, asking for something. Her mother let go of her hand and walked over to greet Kabita, the child waited behind and her big, bright eyes met Kalpana's.

At that moment, Kalpana felt a warm glow inside her heart and she knew that this little girl was the Healer.

"Amrita, come here," her mother said and the little girl scurried over and sat in her mother's lap.

In the next hour, Kabita explained everything to Hari and Bimala— about Amrita being the Healer and Awadesh's capture and Kuruk's plan. "To keep Amrita safe, you have to take her away— to a place without magic. That way, Kuruk won't find her." Kabita concluded.

Hari and Bimala were quiet for some time. Kalpana felt nervous. Would they believe Kabita about something so significant? She was asking them to uproot their entire lives. But surely-- they had to believe her. Afterall, the disappearance of the Healer had been widely discussed on the news all these years and no one had been able to offer an explanation. Did Hari and Bimala know Kabita from before? If they were previously acquainted, perhaps that would help. Their faces had taken a deep, serious expression— etched with fear and apprehension, but Kalpana also detected an unwavering determination to protect their daughter.

Kabita took out the silver locket and handed it to Bimala. "Take this. This locket will help neutralize her powers until she is ready to learn to control it," she said.

Bimala clenched the locket tightly in her hands. "Thank you. We will protect her," Bimala said.

When they had delivered the necessary information, Kabita and Kalpana left.

Two days later, Kalpana came to the house again. She entered through the wooden gate and passed by the garden. Opening the front door, she walked inside.

Everything looked the same as it had two days earlier—all the furniture were in place, the beds were made, utensils were perfectly arranged in the kitchen. But a hushed silence had fallen on the house.

And Kalpana knew that Amrita was gone.

CHAPTER FIVE

RAIN

Present day

Amrita woke up to the sound of falling rain. With the arrival of the daily monsoon rains, summer's heat had subsided, and a cool breeze flowed in from the open window. She lay in bed, awake. The voices of birds, engaging in jubilant morning conversations in the trees outside, seeped into the room. It was quiet besides that.

After a few minutes, Amrita pushed aside her sheets and got out of bed. Without changing, she walked down the wooden staircase. Kalpana was already up, making tea on the kitchen stove. She must have heard Amrita's footsteps, for she asked, "Do you want some tea?"

"Yes," Amrita said and pulled out a chair for herself by the dining table. The wooden table, which could seat four people, was covered on one side with books and papers, leaving the other half unoccupied for Kalpana and Amrita to sit during meals.

During the last stretch of her training as the Healer, Amrita had begun to spend more time at Kalpana's home, learning and practicing the spells. Though her home in the woods was more peaceful to her, she liked being near Kalpana even if going back and forth did not take much time for her. Kalpana had cast a spell around her home to minimize external interference, and that helped.

Living with Kalpana, Amrita had learned many new things about her teacher such as which part of the valley she had grown up in and where she had gone to school. She had been shocked to discover that Kalpana worked as a professor at the local university, because Amrita had always assumed that being her teacher was Kalpana's full time job. In a way, it was. But since Kuruk and the magical community thought that the Healer no longer existed, it was wiser that Kalpana kept the pretense of being a normally employed citizen. Besides, Kalpana loved to teach, so she didn't mind having the side job.

"Here," Kalpana said, placing the milk tea in front of Amrita in her favorite clay cup, which had an engraved sunflower design. Kalpana pulled out another chair and sat down herself, wrapping her hands around the warm mug.

"It is a nice day for tea," Kalpana said, gazing out at the rain slicing through the air. It was an overcast day, and the room was illuminated by the warm, yellow glow of the floor lamp which Kalpana must have turned on in the morning.

Amrita took a sip from her cup, tracing the sunflower design with her fingers. A few seconds later, Kalpana asked, "So how are you feeling today?"

"I'm okay. Just slightly nervous, you know."

"About using the spell?"

"Yes," Amrita said. It always helped to discuss any of her insecurities with her teacher.

"But you've learned it perfectly in the past month. You've aced all the practice drills," Kalpana said, trying to reassure Amrita.

"That's true. But it will still be slightly different, doing it to an actual person."

"Yes. It's a spell that, unfortunately, can't be practiced on an actual person. But you know it well, and you should have no trouble doing it. I believe it," Kalpana said, stressing on the last part.

Amrita nodded, and sipped her tea again.

"And you're sure, this is the right thing to do?" Amrita asked. "I mean about using the spell?"

"Yes, Amrita. It's written in the constitution— when a person abuses their magic in a way that threatens the nation so deeply, the Healer can strip off their magic. That's why the spell was conceived. And Kuruk has committed so many crimes that using the spell would seem merciful to him. I am still reeling about what he did to the Healer before you, Amrita," Kalpana said.

Amrita was quiet for a moment. Yes, Kuruk was a threat to the nation. He was corrupt, he did almost nothing for the country's development, he threatened anyone who tried to stand against him— he was becoming more unhinged as time passed by. And what he'd done to Awadesh— she'd seen all the terrifying details when Dipesh had first come to them. Kuruk's magic was very powerful though— and the thought of facing someone with so much more experience with magic daunted her, even though she was the Healer.

"You've never really had an actual confrontation before. So it can be scary, I understand. But you have to believe in yourself, Amrita," Kalpana said, holding Amrita's hand. "You've come a really long way from when I first met you— I've witnessed your progress. I know you can do this."

Amrita took a deep breath in. It's true that her struggles in the past few years had been massive-- she had even come close to completely giving up once-- but she was grateful that Kalpana had supported her to continue trying. Now that she had achieved control over her magic, she felt content in a way that had been missing her entire life. "Thanks. And you'll be there too, that always makes it better," she said.

Kalpana smiled. "So you have to be mentally prepared too. You know it could be any day that you face Kuruk," Kalpana continued.

"I've been training and practicing a lot, so I should be ok. I'm thinking I should rest today because I've worked hard for the whole week." Amrita said.

Kalpana nodded.

Once Kalpana had decided that Amrita's training was over, with all the spells taught and practiced in the best way possible for a myriad of times, they had planned about how to encounter Kuruk. Amrita, Kalpana and Kabita had decided it would be best if they could get to him alone. Of course Amrita could take on the army of guards Kuruk was always surrounded by, but that was just unnecessary casualty. Encountering Kuruk alone would be most efficient. So, they had decided that Dipesh would try to isolate Kuruk and inform them, and Amrita would apply the spell then.

"Well, let's just wait and see if Dipesh can get Kuruk alone today, and bring him to Satdobato," Kalpana said, getting up from her chair. "I still find it strange that we are relying on Dipesh. But you said he was being honest about helping us, Amrita, so I've agreed to go with the plan."

"He was honest. We can trust him," she reassured. When Dipesh had first come to them, Amrita could see his guilt– his deep remorse about how he had been an accomplice to Awadesh's terrible fate. But stronger had been his determination to set things right. It had taken him so long to overcome his fear of Kuruk, but he finally had. If there was anyone they could rely on now, Amrita knew it was Dipesh.

"Okay then, I'm just going to spend the day doing some work. You can do whatever you'd like. I'll call you when lunch is ready, okay?" Kalpana said.

Amrita nodded and went back up to the guest room, where she stayed at Kalpana's home. It was a small, rectangular room, furnished with a single bed, a closet and a study table. Since Amrita had begun to live here, she had made small changes which were transforming the room into her own. With Kalpana's permission, she had added two paintings onto the previously bare, light blue walls— one of a lush forest and another of the majestic mountains up north. When she first encountered art in the magical world, she had been enchanted— the paintings depicted exquisite artistry, yet there was one detail which captivated her— these pieces of art could move. And so, the painting of the forest had leaves which swayed against a gentle breeze and birds which intermittently came to find shade below the trees, and the painting of the mountains changed as the day did— looking especially magnificent during sunrise and sunset where the snow-capped peaks reflected the orange hues of changing light. Kalpana had added three pots of indoor plants by the window, and the study table had Amrita's books— mostly about magical spells— neatly organized in a bookshelf-like arrangement at the point where the table adjoined the wall. When Amrita was spending time in the room, Kalpana would periodically check up on her— asking if she needed anything or bringing snacks, which mostly consisted of the seasonal fruits, for her long study sessions. Living with Kalpana had been nice; she imagined this is what it would have felt like if she had lived with her mother. And even though she would never get to experience that, this came pretty close.

The rest of the day passed by quietly. Outside, it continued to rain lightly in a soft, silent regularity— only interrupted at times by a sudden burst of rainfall that melted away as fast as it had appeared. Amrita spent the day in her room, reading a book from Kalpana's library about a girl who had lost her home and how she had made a new home amongst the magical community. Amrita had been thrilled to discover that there were works of fiction set in the magical community when she first came to Kalpana's house. Growing up, she had never had many friends so books had filled that void in her life. On evenings and weekends, after she finished her homework, she would settle down on her couch and hours would pass by as she flipped pages after pages which awakened her imagination and lured her into an adventure otherwise unattainable. And so, when she had moved into her house in the woods, she had made sure to take all her books with her. In her new home, Karishma had surprised her with her very own study room that consisted of a magical bookshelf.

Immersed in the story, Amrita lost track of time as the hours of the morning and afternoon melted away. It was evening now, the rain seemed to have temporarily stopped, and the air was cold and fresh— as though celebrating the gift that the rain left as it went by.

The clock pointed to 4:38. She stepped out of her chair and was drinking water, when she heard Kalpana call out, "Amrita, Amrita! Come down, fast!"

Amrita put down her water glass and rushed out the door; she could detect the urgency in Kalpana's voice. Downstairs, Kalpana was standing by the desk, looking at a small rectangular mirror in her hand. On the other hand, she held the traveling locket which she always used to travel to Amrita's home in the woods before.

"What happened?" Amrita asked. She had a pretty good guess.

"It's a message from Dipesh. He's got Kuruk. They're coming to Satdobato. We have to go there now," Kalpana said, preparing to enter the location in the traveling locket.

"Okay, let's go." Amrita said. "You might not need the traveling locket. Since you're going with me," she added hesitantly.

"Yes, you're right," Kalpana said, remembering that the Healer did not require the accessory to travel. Their mind magic meant that they could mentally go to any place, and with a spell, take their bodies there too. Kalpana gripped Amrita's hand and said, "Let's go."

Amrita closed her eyes, and thought of Satdobato. Immediately, she saw a picture of the junction in her mind with the central lotus pond— it looked darker as sunset approached and there were few cars passing by. When she was ready, she said, "*Yatrayam!*"

The next moment when Amrita opened her eyes, she was in Satdobato, Kalpana standing beside her. Here, there was a soft drizzle that felt cool on her body. The sky was streaked with clouds which had absorbed a deep blue color that matched Amrita's blue kurtha. She pushed aside strands of hair that had slipped away from her braid and put them behind her ears. She asked Kalpana, "What do we do now?"

"We just wait. Meanwhile, I think we should create protective barriers on all the road junctions. Leave that one out, because that's where Kuruk is coming from," Kalpana said, pointing at one of the streets.

The two women set to work and within ten minutes six of the seven roads entering the junctions held a transparent barrier that prevented anyone from coming in or going out. Only one road was open through which Kuruk would arrive.

It was silent for a few minutes, the only sound being the rain falling on the lotus pond, creating the distinct, soothing sound of water hitting water. Then, they heard the whirr of an engine and a jeep entered the junction and came to a stop. From the driver's seat, Dipesh stepped out.

Amrita saw Kalpana quickly seal off the gate through which the car had just come. Dipesh walked over to the back seat and opened it.

"You need to step out of the car now," Dipesh said to the man in the backseat.

"Why?" The voice said.

"You'll find out soon," Dipesh said.

Amrita waited. Then, she saw a figure stepping out of the car— dressed in black pants, a white shirt and a matching coat. She couldn't make out his face yet. When he was completely out of the car, he looked around and said, "What is going on?"

For a moment, nothing happened. Amrita was immobile-- the man for whose defeat she had trained for hours and hours was now just a figure in front of her. She could feel his magical energy-- it was strong, yes, but also tainted. Then Amrita stepped forward and said, "Hello, Kuruk."

Kuruk turned behind. From beyond the lotus pond, a young girl was walking towards him. She stopped only a few feet away from him.

Amrita could see his face now. There were lines etched in his face, he looked older, but his eyes were sharp and unyielding. "What is going on?" Kuruk said, looking at Dipesh.

"It's time to pay for what you have done all these years, Kuruk," Amrita said.

"What?" Kuruk said incredulously. "Who is this girl? And why is she saying all these things?" He said to Dipesh.

His trivial attitude towards her began to anger her. She decided to delve deeper into the essence of this man. She closed her eyes.

Suddenly, her mind was inundated with scenes across times and places, and emotions— the unquenchable thirst for power, the heinous crimes committed for that power— scenes of poor men and women begging for change only to be disappointed, of thousands of promises made to citizens but never fulfilled, of corrupt deals made for private gain at the cost of the nation. All these crimes were embedded in Kuruk's consciousness in layers and layers— there were too many moments like them, too many times had he engaged in such depravity. Within a minute, Amrita knew that everything they said about this man was true— this time, he had started the ruin of the nation. Gasping, Amrita opened her eyes.

"You are not worthy of your power Kuruk. You never were. It's time to reinstate justice." Amrita said, walking even closer towards him.

Kuruk laughed. "And you're going to do that? Just get out of here before you hurt yourself," he said and started walking towards the car. "Let's go, Dipesh," he said. But Dipesh did not move.

As Kuruk reached to open the car's door, Amrita raised her hands and with a swift motion, dragged Kuruk back to where he was standing before her. He was taken aback.

"If you attack me like this, I will have to fight back," he said. He raised his hand to cast an attacking spell. But Amrita beat him to it. He extended his arm, said the spell, but nothing happened. She had stopped his attack.

Kuruk was stunned; he could not understand what had just happened. He tried again, more vigorously than before. But Amrita stopped him again and all the energy he had generated to cast the spell knocked him down.

He looked up at the young girl in shock.

"You thought you'd poison my predecessor, ascend to power, and no one would be able to stop you, right?" She said, kneeling down at him.

Then he realized who she was. He gasped. Fear flashed through his eyes.

By now, a significant crowd had gathered around Satdobato. People, realizing that they could not pass through, had stepped out of their cars to see that was going on. They were equally alarmed to see Kuruk lying on the ground before a young, unknown girl.

"You must know what the law says must happen to someone like you, right?" Amrita said, meeting Kuruk's eye level on the ground.

He looked up at her and didn't say anything.

Amrita raised her hand. She closed her eyes, and focused all her energy on Kuruk's magic and connected to it. Then, she said, "*Mokshaya.*"

Soon, a golden light appeared above her hands. It was so bright that Kuruk, Dipesh, Kalpana closed their eyes. Even the bystanders beyond the barrier squinted. Only Amrita could look at it.

Focusing on the light with a fierce gaze, Amrita stood up. Then within seconds, the light of magic turned a deep, black color. And it vanished.

Kuruk opened his eyes again. "No," he whispered, looking at his hands.

"Kuruk Nayan, for crimes against the nation, you will be imprisoned from today. And you probably know by now, but I have used the spell that the constitution mandates for crimes as severe as yours. Your magic has been forfeited."

Amrita walked away from Kuruk, who now was a frail, shivering figure on the road. She walked to Kalpana, who looked triumphant.

"I knew you could do this," she said.

The two women took down the barriers they had set earlier and the crowd of people flooded in, surrounding Kuruk. Everyone was speechless. The fierce tyrant who they had cursed countless times, but had been unable to dethrone, was now lying on the road, helpless. There was a deep silence of disbelief. But a palpable sense of profound relief and triumph also flowed through the crowd. People were gasping, looking at each other with eyes wide open.

Looking at the people around her, Amrita smiled. Then, holding Kalpana's hand, she walked through the crowds, away from the commotion, and the two women vanished into the rain on an empty road.

Glossary Of Spells

1. *Yatrayam*-- A spell used for travel which can only be performed by The Healer. It is derived from the word '*yatra*' which means travel in Nepali.
2. *Jalashaya*-- A spell to release water. It is based on one of the Nepali words for water, '*jal*'.
3. *Sthayitwa ko Mantra*-- Directly translating to 'Spell of Stability', this spell is based on the Nepali word for stability-- *sthayitwa*.
4. *Kholastra*-- A spell to open doors of any kind. It is based on the Nepali word for opening-- '*kholnu*'.
5. *Mokshaya*-- A powerful spell which can only be performed by the Healer and is used to remove magic from a person. It is based on the word '*moksha*' which means liberation.